"I wouldn't blame you if you wanted to quit."

Charles's words jerked her attention back to him as she buckled her seat belt. "Quit? Because someone's accusing you of something for which no one has any proof? I don't think so."

She jumped when his palm hit the steering wheel. "I won't let whoever is doing this send me running with my tail tucked. I won't."

Charles turned, eyes narrowed as he drilled her with the intensity of his gaze. "I didn't kill Olivia Henry. I don't know who did. I just know *I* didn't."

Books by Lynette Eason

Love Inspired Suspense

LYNETTE EASON

makes her home in South Carolina with her husband and two children. Lynette has taught in many areas of education over the past ten years and is very happy to make the transition from teaching school to teaching at writers' conferences. She is a member of RWA (Romance Writers of America), FHL (Faith, Hope, and Love) and ACFW (American Christian Fiction Writers). She is often found online and loves to talk writing with anyone who will listen. You can find her at www.facebook.com/lynetteeasonauthor or www.lynetteeason.com.

THE
BLACK SHEEP'S
REDEMPTION

Lynette Eason

Love Inspired

Special thanks and acknowledgment to
Lynette Eason for her contribution
to the Fitzgerald Bay miniseries.

Recycling programs
for this product may
not exist in your area.

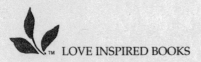

™ LOVE INSPIRED BOOKS

ISBN-13: 978-0-373-67510-4

THE BLACK SHEEP'S REDEMPTION

Copyright © 2012 by Harlequin Books S.A.

www.LoveInspiredBooks.com

Printed in U.S.A.

But we had to celebrate and be glad, because
this brother of yours was dead and is alive again;
he was lost and is found.
—*Luke* 15:32

To my wonderful in-laws, Bill and Diane Eason.
Thank you so much for your love and support.
I couldn't do it without you!

ONE

Demi Taylor jumped as something scraped against the window behind her. Her book fell to the floor. Heart thumping, she bolted from the couch and spun to look at the window. She'd had it cracked to let in the sound of the ocean crashing on the cliffs just below the house but the blinds were closed and blocked her view.

Which was good.

If she couldn't see out, no one could see in. Quickly, she moved the blinds, shut the window and latched it. Heart still racing, she simply stared at it for a moment as she told herself to calm down. Absently, she shoved up her wire-rimmed glasses back on her nose.

What would someone be doing anywhere near that window? Or was she just being silly and it was a tree branch knocking against the pane?

After all, this was her first week on the job as nanny to Charles Fitzgerald's children and she wasn't used to the night sounds of this house. A shiver danced across her skin, raising goose bumps and her blood pressure.

She walked to the front door and checked the lock.

Secured.

Pulling the curtain covering the small window to the left, she parted the blinds and peered out into the dark night. The motion-activated floodlights weren't on which meant no one had moved in front of them.

She breathed a little easier, her heart rate slowed and she could almost laugh at her jumpiness.

It was only eight-thirty. Her new employer should be home any minute. She'd agreed to stay late while he made a house call, but she wasn't sure she liked it.

Ever since waking up in the hospital three weeks ago with no real memory of who she was, or where she belonged, Demi quickly found out she didn't like the dark.

The fact that no one had come forward to identify her even after her face had been all over the news and in the paper was a bitter pill to swallow. Starting over in Fitzgerald Bay, Massachusetts, had seemed like a good idea last week and getting a job almost immediately had seemed like a dream come true.

Now, doubt assailed her.

She peered out again. The inky blackness made her shiver. Charles and his family lived in the

Fitzgerald Bay lighthouse keeper's residence, but even the lighthouse beam didn't reach far enough to cut through the dark.

All Demi knew was that darkness brought flashes of pain, screams, angry words and what she thought was a memory of heavy fists. But that was all she could pull from her shuttered mind before the pounding headache drilled into her, forcing her to abandon her efforts to remember.

No, she didn't like the dark. Add in the weird noises and her adrenaline had stayed spiked since Charles had left three hours ago. A fine tremble set in and she clenched her fingers into fists.

She stood still, eyes closed.

And listened.

Maybe it was just her imagination.

At night, in her small apartment above The Reading Nook bookstore in town, she often thought she heard footsteps outside her door. Lurking, hiding.

But every time she checked, no one was ever there.

Maybe—

Another scrape against the house made her jerk. Then a muffled pop caused her to gasp. What was going on?

This was *not* her imagination.

She made her way into the kitchen and closed the blinds. Standing next to the window with the blinds now shut, she thought she heard a footfall, a rattle.

And another pop.

A muffled curse.

Her breathing quickened once again and her heart picked up speed.

Someone was definitely near the garage.

What should she do? Get the kids? Hide?

The phone.

She needed to call the police.

And Charles.

Trembling, knees almost knocking, she slapped the light switch on the wall and threw the room into total darkness.

A shudder ripped through her as she thought about the children sleeping down the hall. What if the person was trying to get into the house?

She had to protect the children.

Fighting the fear threatening to cripple her, she groped for the handset of the cordless phone on the counter beside the refrigerator.

The cool plastic slid into her palm and she felt for the digits. 9-1-1.

Lifting it to her ear, she waited, heart thudding so hard she wondered if she'd be able to hear the dispatcher.

"9-1-1, what's your emergency?"

"Someone's outside the house," she whispered. "Charles Fitzgerald's home. I think he's trying to get in."

"Ma'am, stay on the line. Can you get somewhere to hide?"

"No. I'm responsible for two children sleeping in two different rooms. If I wake them to hide... The noise they would make... No."

"Someone is on the way, ma'am, just stay on the line."

Demi did as the woman said, while the garage door drew her attention. It was closed, yet she peered out anyway to find the space empty. But the door...

It moved. Rattled.

Sucking in a deep breath, she said, "He's by the garage."

"Help is coming." A pause. "Is Dr. Fitzgerald there?"

"No, I'm his nanny. I'm staying here with the children while he made a house call."

Another pause that seemed like a lifetime. Then, "I've alerted Detective Owen Fitzgerald, Charles's brother, that there's trouble at your location. He's on his way."

"Thank you." Still the fear churned inside her.

More rattling made her spin. Gasp.

Then silence.

Demi stilled.

Was he gone?

She pulled away the phone from her ear and listened. Nothing.

She crossed the kitchen, the moonlight streaming through the blinds lighting her way.

A sound from the direction of the foyer diverted her attention in that direction, and she padded silently toward it. Was he now trying to get in the front door?

Quivering from head to toe, she gulped. Forced herself to keep it together. She had children to protect. She just prayed she'd made the right decision to let them sleep instead of grabbing them and hiding.

Please don't let them wake up, she breathed silently.

Where were the police?

"Please God," she whispered. Then wondered why she found herself praying. She didn't know if she even believed in God. But she wanted to. Wanted to believe He would help her, keep her and the children safe.

Another few seconds passed as she stared at the front door.

Think, Demi, think!

A weapon. She definitely needed a weapon. All she had to do was keep him away from the children long enough for the police to arrive.

But what could she use?

She looked at the block of knives on the kitchen counter and shuddered. The heavy crystal vase would have to do. She grabbed it, ready to hurl it at the head of whoever dared come through the front door.

Then she heard the faint sound of retreating footsteps, moving as though they were in a hurry. She rushed on silent feet to the door and pressed her ear against it.

The distant sound of sirens reached her ears.

Help was on the way.

They must have scared him off.

Relief flowed through her and she nearly dropped the vase from suddenly weak fingers.

Then realized she still held the phone in the other hand.

Demi set the vase on the table, lifted the phone to her ear and said to the 9-1-1 operator still on the line, "The police are close. I can hear their sirens."

"Yes, ma'am."

"I think he left. I heard him run away." Her sentences felt choppy, short. Like she was having trouble stringing coherent thoughts together.

"Don't check, just stay where you are until the police get there."

Demi didn't bother telling the woman she had no intention of opening the door.

The first police cruiser with the Fitzgerald Bay logo on the side finally pulled up to the house.

An officer opened the door and climbed out, weapon drawn, gaze darting.

And then Demi spied Charles's truck pulling up beside the officer.

Demi opened the front door and everyone froze as she stepped outside.

Charles saw his new nanny standing in the doorway and thought his heart would stop. When Owen had called to tell him Demi had dialed 9-1-1 because he had an intruder at his house, his only thought had been to get home and make sure everyone was safe. He couldn't help the terrifying thought that he'd find Demi murdered in his house. Just like Olivia, his former nanny who'd been found dead on the rocks at the base of the lighthouse that was on his property. But Demi wasn't dead. She was standing in front of him, safe and sound.

"Are you all right? The children?" He rushed to her, the limp he'd acquired while serving in Iraq not slowing him one bit. He took in every detail of her appearance. She looked scared and couldn't hide the fine tremor he could see in her hands but, at first glance, she didn't appear hurt.

Her frightened green eyes blinked wide behind her lenses. Her honey-blond hair lay in disarray as though she'd run her hands through it several times. His heartbeat didn't slow.

She nodded. "I'm fine. The children are fine, too. They never woke up."

Owen approached, followed by Charles's other

brother, Deputy Chief of Police Ryan Fitzgerald. Charles introduced them and Ryan asked, "Did you get a look at him?"

Demi shook her head. "I peeked through the blinds, but never saw anyone. He was mostly near the garage door. I did hear some popping sounds, though, and the motion lights never came on."

Owen spoke to the officer next to him. "The garage is around the side of the house. Check it out, will you?"

"Sure." The man's badge read Mike Hughes.

Officer Hughes took off around the side as another patrol car pulled up. Charles groaned when he realized it was his baby sister, Keira, and her partner. Looks like the entire family had gotten the word. But Keira would be the worst. Even though she was the younger sibling, she'd want to mother him. Since Olivia's death and the suspicion that had shadowed his every move, Keira's mothering had turned to smothering.

She climbed from the vehicle, concern etched on her pretty features. "Charles? I was just getting ready to go off duty when I heard the address over the radio. What's going on?"

"We're just about to get to that," Owen said.

"Tell me what I can do to help," Keira offered. "Do I need to stay with the kids?"

"No," Charles assured her. "Demi said they never woke up. They're still sleeping."

Keira ignored him and headed for the front door obviously needing to make sure of that for herself.

Officer Hughes appeared around the corner, a flashlight held at his side. To Demi, he said, "The popping sounds you heard were the lights being broken." To Owen, he jerked his head toward the garage. "I think you need to come see this. And you might want to bring a camera—and another flashlight."

Charles looked at Demi. She said, "I'll stay here out of the way."

He nodded and followed his two brothers and the officer around to the side where his garage was.

As he got a good look at it, he gasped.

In bold red letters, someone had spray painted across the landscape of his garage door.

MURDERER!

TWO

Demi took Officer Hughes up on his offer to listen for the kids. She and Keira followed everyone around to the side of the house to see what all the excitement was about.

She saw the garage door and flinched as though she'd been slapped. Her heart shuddered in pain for the man staring in disbelief at the vandalism. Who would do something like that? Demi hadn't known Charles very long, just long enough to be interviewed and accept the job. She'd heard the rumors. Been privy to the whispers as she walked through town. People wondered how she could work for a suspected murderer. But after meeting Charles, Demi knew in her gut that he hadn't murdered anyone. If she thought he was capable of that, she wouldn't be working for him.

Owen stared at the vile accusation and looked ready to snap someone in two. The set of Keira's jaw said she was right there with Owen.

"What's going on here?"

Demi turned to see Aiden Fitzgerald, chief of police and head of the Fitzgerald family, stride toward his children. She recognized him from the family photo Charles had sitting on his mantel.

"Dad?" Charles frowned. "You didn't have to come out here."

"When I hear someone's trying to break in my son's house, I do." He looked at the garage door and Demi thought she saw him pale when Keira turned her light in his direction. "Someone decided to play dirty tonight, I see."

It wasn't hard to pick up on the fine thread of steel lacing his words.

Charles shook his head. "They egged my house last month and just a couple weeks ago I found all of my tires slashed." He sighed and shrugged. "Don't stress about it, Dad. Until you catch whoever killed Olivia, this stuff is going to happen."

Olivia Henry. Demi had heard the story straight from Charles's mouth. A young woman had come over from Ireland several months ago and Charles had hired her as his nanny. When she'd been found dead on the cliffs at the base of the lighthouse, the town had been rocked.

And then the accusations and rumors had started about Charles's involvement with Olivia.

He'd told Demi in no uncertain terms that there had been nothing between him and Olivia except an employer-employee relationship.

Demi believed him.

"Maybe so," Owen stated, "but that doesn't mean we're just going to sit back and take it."

Keira grunted. "I'm going to check on the kids again."

She disappeared around the corner of the house and Charles simply watched her go.

Demi thought Charles looked weary, battle worn. Not beaten, or defeated, just tired. She ached for him. Wished she could somehow take his pain away. The lump in her throat surprised her. But she couldn't help it. She cared.

She hadn't counted on the spark of attraction that had arched between them when he'd interviewed her.

When Fiona, her landlady and Charles's other sister, had suggested she apply for the nanny position, she'd mentioned he was having trouble finding help because he was a suspect in the murder of his previous nanny. Demi had at first refused. But Fiona had been adamant about her brother's innocence and Demi had finally agreed.

And she'd been captivated by the hurting father accused of a murder he didn't commit. After speaking with him, she had no doubts about his innocence or she wouldn't be there.

Charles's gaze landed on hers. "I'm so sorry."

"It's not your fault," she reassured him.

Stepping to her side, he placed a hand under her

elbow. "Come on. They'll take care of all this. Let me take you home." Right now, she depended upon Charles for most of her transportation to and from his home. She'd love to drive, but had no way of getting a driver's license. Not without some way of identifying herself.

"After she gives a statement," Owen said.

Demi said, "I've told you everything."

"Go through it one more time, if you don't mind," Ryan suggested as he tucked his phone in his back pocket.

"Sure."

They walked back into the house where Keira paced in front of the fireplace. She looked up. "The twins are fine. Still sleeping. I told Officer Hughes he could take off."

"Demi's going to give a statement," Charles said. "Then I'm going to take her home. You said you were just getting ready to go off duty. Do you mind staying with the kids until I get back?"

"I can do that."

Aiden stepped into the house. "I think we've done all we can do here. I'll have a cruiser drive by on a regular basis tonight. We'll talk more tomorrow."

Charles nodded and Demi saw his jaw tighten. "Thanks, Dad."

As Aiden left, Owen flipped his notebook closed. "I'll catch up to you later."

Demi followed Charles out to his car, her heart

chugging with dread. Would he tell her that she no longer had a job?

Then certainty filled her.

No, he wouldn't do that. He needed her. Just like she needed him. Or at least the job. She didn't need *him*.

When she'd arrived in town, she'd had a small bag packed with clothes and some money provided by the sweet nurses who had cared for her after her accident.

Fortunately, she'd run into Fiona Fitzgerald Cobb who'd had a vacant apartment above her shop and was willing to take a chance on someone who didn't have a job and couldn't remember her name.

Getting the nanny job had proven easier than remembering her name. Charles had been desperate. Careful who he hired, but still desperate.

He started the vehicle but didn't move to put it in gear. "I'm afraid I've allowed you to land in a hornet's nest by hiring you. I wouldn't blame you if you wanted to quit."

Charles's words jerked her attention back to him as she buckled her seat belt. "Quit? Because there's a jerk out there trying to intimidate you? Because someone's accusing you of something for which no one has any proof? I don't think so."

The relief on his face made her want to reach out to him, soothe his worry and pain.

She jumped when his palm hit the steering wheel.

"I won't let whoever is doing this send me running with my tail tucked. I won't." Charles turned, eyes narrowed as he drilled her with the intensity of his gaze. "I didn't kill Olivia Henry. I don't know who did. I just know *I* didn't."

Demi gulped. Olivia had been murdered by a blow to the head. And if Demi understood everything she'd managed to pick up from snatches of muttered conversations, not much had been found to prove Charles innocent.

But nothing with substance had been found to prove him guilty, either.

She let her gaze run over him. Dark hair, flashing blue eyes. Honest blue eyes. Hurting blue eyes. But definitely not the eyes of a cold-blooded killer.

Demi said, "I believe you, Charles. I believed you when you offered me the job and explained your situation. And I believe you now."

He closed his eyes and leaned back his head against the headrest. "Thank you for that." He paused. "I'm sorry. You don't deserve this."

Demi couldn't help it. She reached out and curled her fingers around his and squeezed. "It's okay, Charles. I promise. And for the record, I don't think you deserve it, either."

He returned her squeeze then let go to grasp the steering wheel. "I'd better take you home and get back so Keira can get some sleep."

He backed from the driveway and Demi noticed

Ryan standing in the doorway watching them leave. The frown on his face made her blink and she wondered what he was thinking.

After the heavy conversation back at his house, she was ready for a lighter topic. But that wasn't to be when Charles asked, "Any changes in your memory?"

"No." She glanced out the window. "I just continue to have flashes of some things, but nothing I can put my finger on. And if I try too hard, I get terrible headaches."

"Then don't try. It'll happen when it happens. That scab on the edge of your hairline looks pretty bad."

Self-conscious, she raised a hand to touch it. It had mostly healed and she thought it was looking better.

He must have caught her look because he was quick to say, "Hey, I'm sorry, I wasn't saying it looked bad…bad. It was just a medical observation. I just meant that it was obvious that you suffered a pretty traumatic injury."

"Oh." She lowered her hand to clasp it in the other one.

The car slowed and he parked in front of The Reading Nook. The quaint bookstore owned and operated by his sister, Fiona. Demi's apartment was upstairs above the store.

Before she could get out, he said, "Wait a minute, Demi."

She turned expectantly.

He tapped his thumb on the steering wheel then said, "You know, when I interviewed you, the fact that you had amnesia put me off a bit. I mean, how could I trust my children to someone who can't even remember who she is?"

She lifted a brow. "Are you sorry you did?"

"No, of course not." His quick response reassured her. "But I do have a confession to make."

Her brow lifted. "What's that?"

He cleared his throat. "I have to be honest. I had Owen run a background check on you. On the name you gave me, anyway."

She tilted her head. "I figured you probably had. You're not the type to just hand over your children to someone you haven't looked into."

He nodded. "Nothing came up, of course. But more importantly, your fingerprints weren't in the system."

"The nurses in the hospital gave me my last name. I remembered my first name, but that was it." She let out a deep breath. "When I came to in the hospital, the police also tried running my fingerprints. Again, they came up empty, but assured me that might be a good thing. At least I'm not in the criminal database."

At the feeble joke, Charles felt himself smiling.

Another shrug. "I don't blame you for doing a background check on me."

He let out a long sigh. "Good, because I was going crazy feeling like I was lying to you. Part of me was afraid you'd be furious."

"No. I would have done the same thing if the roles were reversed." Her soft voice pulled him to her. Delicate features framed with honey-blond hair drew him like bees to honey. Her emerald-green eyes wanted to ensnare him. Innocence and gentleness radiated from her. He'd definitely made the right choice in hiring her.

"It's only been a week, and the twins already adore you," he said.

A gentle smile pulled at her lips. "The feeling's mutual."

There was something about her that he liked. Trusted. Wanted to know more about.

But not tonight.

"Come on, I'll walk you up." He climbed out of the truck and walked around to help Demi out.

"So, Fitzgerald," the voice to his left said, "is this your next innocent victim?"

THREE

Charles whirled. "Burke, what are you doing here?"

"Just enjoying a little walk. Reveling in my freedom, taking in the taste of the night air." His gaze hardened. "Wondering why criminals are allowed to roam free, given another opportunity to prey on more innocent women."

Burke Hennessy. A lawyer and his father's rival for mayor. Burke and Judge Ronald Monroe, who was rumored to be considering a run for mayor, were two peas in a pod. Fitzgerald Bay would be in major trouble should Burke win the election.

Charles held his tongue long enough to get it under control. Then he said, "Knock it off, Burke. This is Demi Taylor. She's the children's nanny."

"Yes, I'd heard you managed to talk someone into taking the position." Burke smirked and eyed Demi. "Be careful about following in Olivia's footsteps. Especially if they're along the edge of some steep cliffs."

Charles felt his fingers curl into a tight fist. With

effort, he loosened it and forced a smile. He would not sink to this man's level—or do anything to mess up his father's chances to beat Burke in the election. "Nice to see you, too, Burke. Now if you'll excuse us..."

He placed his hand on Demi's rigid back and tried to usher her into the rear entrance of the bookstore.

Burke stepped in front of them, anger smoldering just beneath the surface. Charles felt the tension in his shoulders escalate. Burke jabbed a finger at him. "You know you should be in jail. If the main suspect was anyone else not related to the almighty Fitzgeralds, that person would be rotting in a cell right now."

"And if there were any proof that I'd killed Olivia, I'd be there, family or no family. But there's no proof because I didn't kill her. Get out of the way, Burke. Now."

Demi walked away from the two of them, pulling her keys from her purse. Charles swallowed hard. Was she scared? Repulsed? Had she decided Burke was right and that she was placing herself in danger by just being in his company?

He remembered the look in her eyes when she'd said she believed him. No, it was something else.

Turning his back on Hennessy, Charles followed Demi. He saw her hands shaking as she unlocked the door and slipped inside.

"You haven't heard the last of this, Fitzgerald!" Burke hollered.

Charles didn't bother to turn around and waste any more time or breath on the man. "Demi?" She stopped on the steps and looked back down at him. The fear in her eyes cut him. "Hey, I'm so sorry."

"No. Don't apologize. It wasn't you," she said with a shudder. "I had a flash of something. Of violence and anger and…and I just had to get away from that man."

Charles hurried up to her and put a hand on her shoulder. "I understand. I was in a bit of a hurry to get away from him myself."

"Is he gone?"

"Yes, I think so. I didn't stick around to make sure."

She took a deep breath and lifted a brow. "Too busy trying not to smash his nose?"

Charles jerked then gave a surprised laugh. "You noticed?"

"Oh, yeah. I noticed." He felt some of the tension leave the shoulder under his hand. She bit her lip then said, "I'm sorry I was such a wimp. I didn't mean to just walk away and leave you to deal with him, I just…"

He placed a finger on her lips. Her soft lips.

He pulled back his finger and rubbed it with his thumb even as he said, "No need to apologize. Burke's a pain with a loud mouth, but he's harmless. The trick is to just ignore him."

She nodded and finished the trek up the steps. At the top, she turned down the short hallway that led to her apartment.

Charles caught her before she got to the door. "Demi, I want to make something really clear."

"Sure, what is it?"

He raked a hand through his hair. "The rumor is that Olivia and I were romantically involved." A frown creased her forehead and he resisted the urge to smooth the shallow lines. "We weren't. She was my children's nanny and I trusted her with my children. She was a pretty private person, but I'd like to think we were becoming friends. There were no romantic feelings between us whatsoever."

Her eyes stayed locked on his for the longest time and he wanted to squirm under the scrutiny, but he didn't. He just stood there as she decided whether she believed him or not.

Finally, she smiled. "I believed you the first time you told me that. Tonight hasn't changed anything."

Key ready, she reached out to unlock the door when Charles stopped her again, his hand on hers. "Wait a minute. It's open."

Demi gripped the keys tighter and pulled back. "That's weird."

"You probably just didn't pull it shut behind you hard enough when you left earlier."

The doubt on her face said she wasn't buying it.

And after the night he'd just had, he wasn't sure he was, either.

* * *

Demi stared at the door. "Maybe Fiona needed to get in for some reason." But why? And why would she leave the door open? "The furniture was delivered last week. Maybe they had something else to bring up…or…or…something."

And what about Chloe, the stray cat she'd taken in the day she'd moved into the apartment? Chloe had followed Demi up the stairs and sat outside the door meowing until Demi had finally let her in. Chloe had made herself at home and some of Demi's loneliness had dissipated.

Had Chloe slipped out the open door?

Worry for the cat and other emotions swept through her.

Unexplainable fear.

Breath-stealing panic.

Something flashed in her mind. A clenched fist, a harsh yell. Pain lancing through her head. She blinked, raised a hand to her forehead, felt the scar.

Then the image was gone, leaving a pounding headache in its wake.

"Demi? What is it? What did you remember?"

"Fear," she blurted out. "Just a horrible fear, but I don't know the source. I don't know why!" She lifted a hand to her head and pressed as though she could push the headache out and the memories back in.

He pulled her to him while she shook. His arms held her, comforted her. Offered her shelter.

Swallowing, her breath hitched as she gathered herself and pulled away to face the door once more.

"I'm okay." Her hand reached out to push the door open. She appreciated Charles's comforting presence behind her. "You're probably right," she said, hating the tremble in her voice, but unable to do anything about it. "I'm sure I just didn't close the door tight." From what she could see, all looked normal. Except...

"Chloe?" she called softly. "Here, kitty."

Demi stepped inside for a better look in the kitchen. "Everything looks fine in here. But my cat usually greets me when I come in."

She moved to the small living area, Charles right behind her. It was just as she'd left it. The new couch hugged the far wall with the afghan Fiona had given her bunched up against one end. The coffee table held the latest book she'd been reading. Her morning's coffee cup sat on a coaster on the end table.

Normal.

But where was Chloe?

Her pulse slowed and her breathing evened out. But sorrow hit her. If Chloe was gone, Demi knew she would miss the cat who, for the most part, had been her only company in the evenings for the past week.

She walked the few steps to the bedroom and peeked in. All looked fine. Just as she was about to check under the bed for the missing feline, her gaze landed on the closet door.

It was shut.

"What is it?"

Charles's voice in her left ear made her jump. He'd picked up on her sudden stillness.

"The closet's shut." She pushed her wire-rimmed glasses up on her nose.

"And that's a bad thing?"

"It was open this morning when I left to take care of the kids."

Why could she remember that and not her last name? Regardless, she distinctly remembered leaving it open. Heart thudding, sweat broke out on her upper lip.

Her front door had been cracked open. Had someone been in the apartment? Someone looking for something? For her?

Go, get away. Run.

Fear resurrected its head and cut off her breath. But why? Why did she feel this fear that seemed to come from nowhere? There had to be a reason. *Why* couldn't she remember?

"Maybe we should just leave," she said. "Something's not right here."

He placed a hand on her shoulder and the comfort it offered made her shiver. "Let me just check the closet for you."

"No!"

And the images hit her again. A flash of blood, a heavy hand on her face. Someone screaming. Was that her?

She gasped, her breaths came in pants and that sweeping fear that came from a place she couldn't explain nearly consumed her.

Shaking with the urge to flee, she stepped back never taking her eyes from the closet door.

"Demi." His gentle voice forced her gaze to his. Gulping, she saw concern, caring…a warmth that thawed the ice freezing in her veins. "Let me check," he insisted. "It's fine. Really. If someone was in there, I feel sure he would have made his presence known by now."

Pulling in a deep breath, she nodded. Then firmed her jaw.

Walking to the end table, she picked up the lamp and stepped back to the closet door. "All right, I'm ready."

"What are you doing?"

"If someone's in the closet, I'm not leaving you to fight him alone."

The tightness along his jawline that never seemed to ease, finally did. He smiled and nodded. Then his expression turned hard again as he eyed the closet.

Charles walked to the closet and swung open the door, even as he crouched in a defensive position ready for whatever might come at him. A cat darted out, startling him.

His pulse pounded and he realized how tightly wound his nerves were. Of course after what he'd come home to tonight, it wasn't a surprise. And then Burke's confrontation in the alley...

He watched Demi set the lamp back on the table then lean over to snag the cat and hold her close. "Silly cat, how did you get locked in there?"

"Is the window open? Maybe there was a draft and it blew the door shut."

Demi walked over to the only window in the small room and pushed back the curtains. "No. It's closed."

"Well the cat didn't close herself in the closet." He shrugged. "I don't know. It is kind of strange, I'll admit, but maybe someone from the bookstore wandered upstairs, found your door and opened it to see what was behind it. Seeing that it was an apartment, maybe the person didn't quite shut the apartment door well enough and the draft caused the closet door to shut."

Demi lifted a brow at the weak suggestion. Charles grimaced. "Yeah, I'm not really buying that, either."

Demi's frown deepened. "I suppose something like that could have happened. But I'm pretty sure I locked the apartment door when I left earlier." Reaching inside the closet, she flipped on the light switch.

He could see the sum total of her wardrobe. Four

or five shirts. Three pairs of jeans, two pairs of shorts and a sweatshirt and a light windbreaker. On the floor, there were a pair of sandals and some pink slippers. She wore her only pair of tennis shoes.

The sparse selection stunned him. He thought about his ex-wife and her bursting-at-the-seams closet. He'd always been tripping over her shoes that seemed to multiply daily.

And then there was Demi.

Charles felt his heart ache for the fragile-looking woman who'd been victimized twice in one night.

Demi saw the pity in Charles's eyes and turned away from it. She wasn't ashamed of her lack of material goods and she didn't need anyone feeling sorry for her. Straightening her back, she firmed her jaw. Another look around confirmed what she'd originally thought. "Nothing's missing."

"You're sure?"

For some strange reason, Demi felt like giggling. "Trust me, I'm sure. I have no jewelry, no fancy clothes, nothing. There's nothing worth stealing."

Charles's stare made the back of Demi's neck heat up. Ignoring the sensation and praying the flush didn't spread to her cheeks, Demi looked around. "Everything looks fine. I guess no one was up here after all." She frowned, not understanding how this could be when the closet door was shut. "I'll ask Fiona if she came up here. If she didn't, then—" she lifted her shoulders in a shrug "—I have no explanation."

"Is there any reason someone would want to break into your home?"

"No." She paused. "At least I don't think so…I mean…" she stammered to a halt. How would she know? "I don't really know."

"Of course there is," he muttered answering his own question. "Someone who might be mad that you're working for me. Maybe this is just the beginning."

Demi came to his side. "Stop it."

He looked at her. She frowned at him and he could see the frustration in her eyes. Charles sighed. "You're right. I don't need to be having a pity party. But I hate to think of you being in danger because of me." He paused. "Will you be all right to stay here alone?"

Her chin jutted out. "Of course. Nobody was here. I'm just being jumpy after what happened at your house." She glanced at the clock on the wall. "You'd better head home. I'm sure Keira is tired from working all day and is ready to spend some time in her own house."

Charles rubbed his chin, wanting to protest. But he knew she was right. Again. "Okay." He walked to the door then turned. "Tomorrow's Saturday." He found himself fidgeting with the doorknob and forced his hands to his side. "I know it's your day off, but…ah…how would you feel about spending it with me and the kids?" He wanted to spend more time with her. Getting to know her better was at the top of his priority list. At first he tried to tell himself it was because of the kids, but if he was honest, he'd admit he wanted to get to know her better…for himself.

Demi swallowed. Hard. Excitement swirled in the pit of her stomach even as she wondered if spending the day with her boss—her very attractive boss—was a wise thing to do.

Probably not.

"Sure," she said. "I'd love that."

His shoulders relaxed and when he smiled, his blue eyes crinkled at the corners. "Great. I'll let Brianne and Aaron know. They'll be thrilled."

What about you? she wanted to ask. But bit her lip in time to keep the words from spilling out.

"Nine o'clock?" he asked.

"I'll be ready."

She shut the door behind him and made sure the lock clicked. She would definitely be ready to spend the day with them, but wondered if she would get any sleep at all.

Looking around, seeing nothing out of place, she wondered what she was missing.

Because no matter what she had said to the contrary, she felt sure someone had been in her apartment.

FOUR

Saturday morning dawned a little overcast, but no rain fell yet. The thought of the day to come sent a twinge of excitement through Demi, spurring her to toss back the covers and pad toward the bathroom. She had something to do today besides sit in her apartment spilling her guts to Chloe and bemoaning the fact that her memory hadn't returned yet.

Self-pity was no fun. It was time to start making plans for the future, start to live again and try to either get her memory back or accept that it was gone for good and move on.

Of course she wanted her memory back, but if that wasn't meant to be, she was determined not to let the amnesia negatively affect the rest of her life.

At least that was the pep talk for this morning. Tonight, when she was all alone once again, she would have to figure out how to keep the despair and frustration at bay.

Briefly, she thought about the Bible she'd seen on the shelf in the bookstore. Maybe she should turn to God for comfort. Making a mental note to think about that, she went into the kitchen for her morning cup of coffee.

And realized she didn't smell it.

Another thing she'd discovered since getting out of the hospital was that she loved coffee. Any kind, flavored, black, with cream. It didn't matter.

The last thing she did before bed was set the timer on the coffeemaker Fiona had given her as a housewarming gift.

Only she'd been so distracted last night, she'd forgotten to set the timer.

She filled the carafe then opened the cabinet to pull out the canister of coffee.

When she pulled off the top, she gaped.

A piece of paper sat on top of the ground coffee.

Wariness flooded her. How did this get in her coffee can? Reaching in, she pulled it out and read, *Stay away from Charles Fitzgerald. You don't belong here.*

Knees suddenly week, she dropped the paper back into the can, slapped on the top and gasped, her lungs deflated.

Flashes of a hard fist. Shouted angry words. Pain in her head.

She cried out and sank to the floor, hands gripping her hair. Her head throbbed, but she forced herself to think, to remember.

"No!" The word echoed, the pain in her head intensified and tears slipped down her cheeks. Heart thudding, head pounding, she whispered, "Please, stop. Stop."

For the next few minutes she sat there and emptied her mind of every thought. She couldn't force it. And she had to pull herself together for Charles and the children.

Twenty minutes later, a fine tremor still shook her, but she took a look in the mirror as she ran a brush through her hair. The excited anticipation of the day had waned because of the message still in her coffee can—and the disturbing flashes that resonated in the corners of her mind.

But the thing holding her together was the thought of being with Charles and the children.

That gnawing in the pit of her stomach agitated her as she realized she'd been right. Her instincts had been dead-on when she thought someone had been in the apartment yesterday.

But who?

And what should she do with the odd—and scary—message? Was it from someone who was warning her away from Charles because of what happened to Olivia? But what a weird way to do so.

Should she report it to the police? But what could they do? And why say she didn't belong there? Why would someone go to all the trouble to sneak into her apartment and leave that in her coffee can?

The coffee can.

A strange place for a note. Why put it there?

Unless the person knew her. Knew her habits.

A chill swept through her.

The person had to know that she loved coffee. That she would be in that coffee can first thing this morning. Or soon anyway.

Or was it simply coincidence? The coffeemaker sat in plain sight on the counter. It would be a short thought to realize there would be coffee in the cabinet somewhere.

But *why?*

Her head started to ache again. Determined to push the incident out of her mind until she felt ready to deal with it, she focused on the excitement she'd felt when she first woke up and remembered what she was doing for the day.

She muttered, "You really shouldn't be so excited about spending the day with Charles and the kids. He's your employer, nothing more."

She flushed as she said the words out loud because she knew they were a lie.

She'd been attracted to him the minute she'd looked into those blue eyes and seen compassion— and a spark of something more as he'd questioned her during the interview for the nanny position.

Wishing she had some lip gloss or lipstick made her flush hotter and she rolled her eyes at her reflection. Shiny lips hadn't gotten her the job. Trustworthiness and capability were the qualities Charles had been looking for, and she'd assured him that she had both. He was obviously a good father who was very careful about whom he left his children with.

As well he should be.

But today wasn't about work even though she looked forward to caring for the children during their time together. Most of all, she wanted to get to know Charles a little better. Spending the day together would allow that.

She didn't mind the idea one bit.

But someone else did. Someone else thought she didn't belong here. Here in town? Here with Charles? Here in The Reading Nook?

Again, who?

Standing at the window in her bedroom, she glanced down in the small alley that ran behind her building. It was a shortcut to the other street and had a lot of traffic most days.

She'd stood in this spot many times since moving in. Just watching, wondering about the lives that passed under her window.

Today, the foot traffic was light.

A solitary figure in a hooded sweatshirt, hands tucked in the front pockets walked slowly. Then paused in front of the back door that would lead into her building. She watched him reach out, his arm moved in a twisting motion.

What was he doing?

Seeing if the door was unlocked?

Fortunately, she and Fiona kept it locked unless there was a delivery expected. Tensing, she waited to see if he could get in. Was he the one who'd broken in and left the note?

When he dropped his hand and turned to walk off, she breathed a sigh of relief.

Chloe wound herself around Demi's left ankle, distracting her from her thoughts and unanswered questions. She picked up the cat and carried her to the bed. Setting the animal on the coverlet, she asked, "Shorts or jeans?"

Chloe commenced cleaning her left front paw.

"Right. That's what I thought, too. Jeans it is."

Pulling up her hair into a ponytail, Demi dressed in her thrift store jeans and a flowered top. She opened her purse and grabbed a ten-dollar bill that she stuffed into her front pocket.

She picked up the cell phone Charles had insisted she have the first day she'd reported for work and stuck that in her back pocket. Then she snatched her light jacket from the closet. Unable to bring herself to close the door, she left it cracked open.

Demi stepped out into the hall and pulled the apartment door tight behind her. She double-checked the lock, doing her best to push yesterday's and this morning's incidents from her mind. Shivering at the unpleasant memories, she pocketed the key and slipped into her jacket.

Once down the steps and outside, she looked

around for the man who'd stopped at her building and tested the doorknob. Seeing no one, she told herself to relax.

Since she was much too early to meet Charles and the twins—and there was no way she was touching that coffee in her cabinet—Demi decided to have breakfast at the Sugar Plum Café. Excitement at seeing Charles again swirled through her. And yet she couldn't help wonder at the reasons behind the invitation. Did he just want extra help with the twins? Or was it possible he was interested in her as a woman and a potential date? She grimaced. It would do no good to ask questions she didn't have the answers for. "Just take it one day at a time," she whispered.

Clouds hung low and gray, but the sun peeped out behind them so she hoped the rain would hold off long enough to enjoy the day with the Charles Fitzgerald family.

After several glances up and down the street, she crossed at the intersection, then followed the short road past the park. Splashing through a puddle left over from the night rain, she finally found herself in front of the café. The white structure with the large porch was welcoming. And yet, she couldn't shake the feeling that someone was watching her. Waiting for her.

But who? And why?

The man she'd seen trying to get in the building?

Demi scoffed at herself. He was probably someone who wanted to go to the bookstore and thought he could take a shortcut by going in the back door.

Surely that was all it was.

But what about the note?

Still feeling a hovering sense of foreboding, Demi shivered as she stepped inside and took in the atmosphere. One of comfort and refuge with tables and chairs and couches. The display of pictures tacked to the walls was mind-boggling. Everywhere one looked, a picture smiled back.

Several patrons sat alone, working on laptops. Tempting smells made her empty stomach rumble and she headed straight for the glass-front case display. An assortment of cakes and pastries called to her. She wanted one of each, but she'd only been working for one week and her funds were still tight.

"Can I help you?"

Demi jumped and turned to see a pretty woman in her late twenties. Her brown eyes sparkled friendliness. Victoria, the owner of the Sugar Plum Café.

After checking the prices on the menu posted on the wall, Demi chose the cheapest option. "I'd love a cup of coffee, black, please."

"Sure thing." In a few minutes, Victoria returned and handed her the cup. "So how are things going?"

"Pretty well."

"Charles hired you to be the children's nanny, didn't he?"

"I guess it's all over town by now."

"Indeed. I'm just glad you're not buying into all that nonsense about Charles killing Olivia."

"No. I'm not buying into it."

From what Demi understood, Olivia had come to Fitzgerald Bay from Ireland three months before her murder, a stranger in town, but one who quickly made friends with Victoria and her daughter, Paige, when she'd stayed at the inn.

Curiosity lifted Victoria's brow. "So, you work for my future brother-in-law, but I don't really know anything about you. Do you have family around here?"

Victoria was engaged to Owen Fitzgerald, Charles's younger brother and a detective with the police force.

"I…" What could she say? *I don't know? I don't remember?* Demi forced a smile as she handed over three precious dollars. "No. I'm just looking for a new start. Fitzgerald Bay seemed like the kind of place where I could find that."

"You're right about that. Why don't you have a seat over there by the fire? It may be May, but it's still chilly here first thing in the morning so I keep the fire going."

Demi nodded. "Thanks. I'll do that." She started toward the comfy-looking chair by the flickering flames.

Once seated, she grabbed the abandoned newspaper on the table before her and opened it. Of course the front page story was still about Olivia Henry's unsolved murder. The first murder in forty years in this town. But there was nothing about the incident at Charles's house last night. She shivered and set the paper back on the table.

The fire crackled and the warmth felt lovely. Soon, she'd warmed up enough to shrug out of the light jacket one of the nurses had given her before she'd been discharged from the hospital three weeks ago.

Everything she now owned in the world had been given to her by another person. The familiar fear filled her, coming from a place she couldn't define. She just knew it was very real. A mental picture of the note in her coffee grounds added to that feeling. Someone had been in her home. Warning her to stay away from Charles.

She couldn't fathom it. But *who? Who?*

And should she report it?

But what would she say? What could the police do about it? She continued to toy with the idea. Maybe she would tell Charles about it and see what advice he had to offer. Then again, if she told Charles, that would just add to his guilt about hiring her. What if he fired her because he thought it would keep her safe?

She shuddered. Jobs in Fitzgerald Bay were few and far between. She couldn't afford to lose the nanny position. No, she'd just keep quiet about the note and hope Olivia's murderer was found soon.

Demi briefly wondered if she should pray about everything. Did she even know how?

Dear God, please give me my memories back. I need to know who I am. I need to know why I'm so afraid and constantly feeling like I need to watch my back... Please....

Closing her eyes, she did her best to bring forth memories from before she woke in the hospital.

And couldn't do it. Not even one. Just the feeling of fear whenever she tried to remember.

And the headache.

And now the note in her coffee can. The headache worsened.

Quickly, she tossed her thoughts in another direction.

Fitzgerald Bay. A small close-knit community that was friendly to outsiders. At least that's what the website advertised when she'd been narrowing down her choices.

And now she had a place to live and a good job. She was doing all right for someone who'd had nothing and no one three weeks ago.

She glanced at the clock on the wall behind the counter. Eight forty-five. She still had a few minutes before she needed to walk to the park. Demi leaned her head against the cushioned back of the chair and stared out the window while she sipped her coffee.

Her mind spun, wondering, desperate to remember who she was, where she was from, if she had relatives that missed her. She swallowed hard against the tears that sprang to the surface.

"Hey."

Demi jumped and did her best to hide her whirling emotions from Victoria who stood before her holding a plate of sandwiches and some delicious-looking pastries.

"Oh. Sorry, I was…thinking."

Victoria set the plate on the table beside Demi and said, "Help yourself."

"What? Oh, no, that's okay. I have money." She flushed and wondered if she looked like a charity case.

Victoria shrugged. "I just thought I'd give you a sampling of what we serve here. Maybe tempt you to come back."

Now Demi felt embarrassed. And hungry. "Well, thank you." She snitched a croissant filled with chicken salad and took a bite as she tried to push the depressing thoughts from her mind. "Wow. This is delicious. I'll definitely be back."

They laughed and Victoria said, "It's my own chicken salad recipe. Pretty good, huh?"

"You could win ribbons with this stuff." Demi quickly polished off the first sandwich and took a sip of coffee.

Victoria laughed. "I knew I liked you." She settled into the chair opposite Demi. "So, how do you like working for Charles? I know it's been only one week, but you must have some impressions."

What was the woman fishing for? "I'm very grateful he hired me. The children are definitely a handful, but very precious."

"I know. They're great. And Charles is a wonderful man regardless of what you might hear said around town."

"Oh, come on, Victoria, how can you say that?"

Demi and Victoria turned in unison to find the owner of the voice. A young woman with her blond hair hanging around one shoulder planted her hands on her hips. "Charles might be guilty of murder."

Victoria sighed. "Meghan Henry, cousin to Olivia Henry, meet Demi Taylor."

Demi gave the adamant young woman with the pretty hazel eyes a tremulous smile. "Hi."

"Hi. I'm sorry, I shouldn't have interrupted your conversation, but I'm just very concerned for you. For anyone who has anything to do with Charles Fitzgerald." And she did look worried, a genuine kind of worried, not the fake kind of worried most people in the town had expressed in order to pump her for information about the Fitzgeralds.

Frowning, Demi exchanged a look with Victoria then said, "I appreciate your concern, but Charles has been nothing but kind to me."

Meghan sighed. "Well, I would watch my back if

I were you." She slipped her purse over her shoulder. "I'm in the cottage on the beach, the one just up from the lighthouse. If you ever need anything, please come see me."

Again, sincerity rang in Meghan's words and Demi wasn't sure what to think. "Well, thank you. I appreciate that."

"Be careful, okay?" She glanced between her and Victoria. "See you around."

With that, she left.

Demi raised a brow at Victoria who sighed. "I hope you won't take what she said to heart. I don't believe for a minute that he murdered Olivia."

"I know. I don't believe he did, either."

"Good." Approval radiated from the woman. "He's needed some help for a long time. His father's housekeeper, Mrs. Mulrooney, is wonderful, but she can't keep up with two rambunctious toddlers. I'm so glad Charles found you."

Demi felt a smile slip across her face. "Thanks. It was actually his sister Fiona who told me about the job." She looked at the clock again. "And now I've got to run. Nice to meet you."

"You, too. I'm sure we'll be seeing a lot of each other."

Charles gave the swing a push and felt his heart lighten at his children's laughter. His eyes drifted from his kids to the direction he knew Demi would come from.

He'd had a hard time falling asleep last night as her image kept appearing in his thoughts—in between wondering who'd vandalized his house. He preferred thoughts of Demi. She was beautiful, had a gentle spirit about her—and she scared him to pieces.

She'd been in his life just a short time, but already, he felt as though he'd known her for a while. And while it was true he didn't know as much as he'd like due to the amnesia, he liked what he knew, what he'd observed.

He also knew that if he had any brains at all, he'd find a woman old enough to be his mother to care for the children simply to cut down on the wagging tongues. Unfortunately, no one in that age category seemed to be in the market for a job that taxing. Or one that had anything to do with him.

Him. A murder suspect. He couldn't wrap his mind around it. But apparently the townspeople didn't have any trouble believing it. Everywhere he went, he felt eyes on him, knew they were wondering if he was a killer. His medical practice had suffered as had his confidence in most of those he used to call friends.

His gaze went to a young couple strolling hand in hand along the park path as though they didn't have a care in the world. He remembered those days. Sometimes he missed them. Then he looked at Brianne and Aaron and wouldn't change the past even if he could.

His eyes went back to The Reading Nook bookstore.

But Demi had him thinking more and more about the future and what it might be like to find the one he was supposed to spend the rest of his life with.

A feeling of someone watching pulled him from his thoughts. Glancing around, Charles spotted two women on a park bench near the sandbox. They stared at him as they talked.

Christina Hennessy and Dolores Nunez, nanny for Burke and Christina's toddler. Distaste curled through him. He didn't care for Mrs. Hennessy much, not simply because she was Burke's wife, but because she was such a fake. Probably why she and his ex, Kathleen, had gotten along so well.

And still, she didn't take her gaze from him. Out of a morbid sense of humor, he lifted a hand and waved.

Her right brow rose and she deliberately ignored him, turning her gaze on the nanny.

Why the woman needed a nanny was beyond him. She didn't work and didn't seem to have any responsibilities that he could see.

Speaking of nannies, Demi surprised him and stepped out of the Sugar Plum Café instead of The

Reading Nook and headed his way. He tried to forget about the pair across the park.

But the hair on the back of his neck rose as he continued to feel their stares. He reminded himself not to let their snide glances and whispered words affect him.

But a small part of him wanted to stomp across the park and demand they cease their nasty gossip. Instead, he took a deep breath and watched Demi approach. The concerned frown on her features told him that she'd picked up on his expression. With effort, he loosened his jaw and relaxed his shoulders.

Only to tense up again when Burke stepped into view. The man glanced at him and pursed his lips as though seeing something distasteful.

He said something to Christina and the nanny, then practically shouted, "Come on. It's not safe for Georgina to play here. Apparently, they don't screen the people who use this place and will allow murderers around small children."

FIVE

Demi couldn't read the expression on Charles's face, but the smile he shot her looked forced, the frown lines between his brows deeper than yesterday.

Burke said something that Demi wasn't close enough to catch, but apparently Charles heard it—and didn't like it. She saw the fury on his face and the rock-hard tension in his body. She had a feeling he was exercising extreme self-control at the moment.

Burke held his daughter as he and the two women left the park.

Charles relaxed and occupied himself by pushing the twins on the swings. They each sat in the little side-by-side bucket seats, legs dangling. Sweet laughter reached her ears, chasing away the frown she knew was on her face.

A twinge in the vicinity of her heart made her wince. What about her own father? Where was he? Was he missing her? Worried about her? Or was he even alive? She had the same questions about her mother, but no amount of trying could bring to mind a face that she could call family.

Drawing in a deep breath, she stuffed her sorrow away and pasted a smile on her face. "Good morning," she called.

Charles turned and his answering smile flashed her way. It seemed a little less forced than the previous one. "Hey, there. We got here a bit early and this was the only way I could corral them."

Demi let out a laugh. "Looks like fun."

"They seem to like it, but even as petite as you are, I don't think you'd fit in the seat."

His appreciative gaze made her pause. Was he flirting with her? Sure looked like it. Did she mind? Warmth centered itself in her midsection. No, she didn't mind a bit. "You're silly." She stepped next to him, placing herself behind Aaron. "Let me take one so you don't have to dance back and forth between them."

His eyes lingered on her a moment longer and his expression seemed to soften even more. "That'd be nice. Thanks."

Demi waited until the little boy came back toward her then gave him a gentle push. He squealed and laughed, his black hair blowing in the wind. As he approached her again, he held out his hand and yelled, "I gots Dino!"

Demi laughed and caught the swing, pulling

Aaron to her so she could study the plastic dino-
saur clutched in his fingers. "He's the best-looking
dino I've ever seen."

That sent Aaron into more peals of laughter. She
let the swing go and Aaron swooped into the air.

She looked at Charles who stood watching her,
the strangest expression on his face. "What?" she
asked.

He shook his head and cleared his throat. "Nothing really. You're just good with them." He smiled.
"So, how are you this morning?"

"I'm…" She started to say fine, then decided to be
honest. "I had a rough night." And a crazy morning.
"But I suppose that was to be expected after that
scare I had at your house, then thinking someone
was in my apartment." She didn't bother to mention
the man she thought had tried to get into the building through the back door. And she didn't want to
say anything about the message in her coffee can.
Not yet. She didn't want to ruin what had the potential to be a wonderful day.

"I'm sorry."

Demi shrugged and gave the swing another push.
Aaron crowed, "Higher!"

She complied then looked at Charles. His blue
eyes sparkled when he watched his children. Instead she asked another question burning in the
back of her mind. "Do you mind me asking where
the twins' mother is?"

He went still for a moment then let out a sigh before giving Brianne another push. "No, it's not like it's a secret or anything. Kathleen left me when the twins were about six months old." He shook his head. "Her parents spoiled her and she always was rather flighty, I suppose, but…" He shrugged. "She seemed to love me and I…well…I was enamored with her." He pulled in a deep breath. "And then after the babies came, she just couldn't handle it. I was in the process of hiring a nanny to help her out. One day Kathleen was there, the next she was gone. Months later, she sent me divorce papers and a note that she was living in Mexico fulfilling her dream of becoming an artist and wanted to get married to another man, an artist who understands her."

All Demi could think was that the woman was insane. She'd given up all this for…that? "I'm so sorry. That must have been a terrible time."

"It was." Pain flashed across his face. "But you know, I don't really hurt for me anymore. It is what it is. I just hurt for them." He nodded toward the kids. "It's going to be hard explaining her desertion when the time comes."

Demi bit her lip. "Yeah."

"Then again, if that's the kind of person she's decided to be, maybe they're better off not knowing her." He paused. "Would you like to take the kids down to the beach?" Charles asked. "It's too cold to get in the water, but we could build a sand castle and let them run around, burn off some energy, maybe get some ice cream."

Brianne heard him and grinned. "Ice cream."

"I like chocolate," Demi said. "What's your favorite?"

"Ice cream, Daddy!"

Charles groaned. "Now I've done it."

"What?"

"I'll have to let her have some ice cream or I'll hear about it all night."

"Ice cream! Now!" Brianne shouted.

"Hush, Bri, not so loud. We'll get some in a little while. Why don't we go play in the sand?"

"No sand. I want some ice cream."

Charles tossed Demi a wry look. "We might be eating ice cream a little earlier than I planned."

Swings, the park, the beach and now ice cream? Shivers danced up her arms. This day was feeling more and more like a date.

She looked at him, wanting to ask him to clarify if this was a date or if they were just…hanging out. Instead, she simply said, "That sounds nice."

Ten minutes later, the twins were in their car seats in the back of Charles's truck. The red king cab with the leather seats was plush and roomy. Demi inhaled the new-car scent and smiled. "How long have you had this?"

Charles closed his door and cranked the engine. "A couple months."

"I like it."

He flashed her a grin. "I do, too."

Small talk filled the short ride to the beach, interrupted occasionally by Aaron and Brianne's two-year-old chatter.

Charles looked in the rearview mirror and frowned. His eyes flicked back to the road in front of him. Then up to the mirror.

"What's wrong?"

"That car's coming up behind us pretty fast."

Demi glanced in the side mirror and spied a dark-colored sedan gaining on them. "Maybe he's in a hurry and will go around."

Charles let his foot off the gas and slowed.

And the car kept coming. Demi shifted, uneasy. "Charles?"

Charles's fingers flexed on the wheel. The narrow two-lane road didn't leave a lot of room to maneuver and she wondered what he was thinking.

Another look in the mirror showed the car about twenty feet behind them. Ten.

"Charles! He's going to hit you!"

"Hold on." He pressed the gas pedal. Aaron, picking up on the tension, started to cry.

The truck growled to life, responding to the burst of speed instantly. The sedan fell back, but soon gained lost ground.

"I don't want to go too much faster, there's a curve just ahead," Charles said.

"Can you turn off?"

"Hang on, he's coming faster."

Demi felt herself jerk forward, then slam back. She yelped. Brianne cried out and Aaron howled.

Charles went faster. "Call 9-1-1. Tell them where we are."

The curve ahead was sharp, the guardrail offering flimsy protection against a speeding vehicle.

Demi clutched the door and held on while her heart thumped in terror. She held the phone to her ear with effort. The operator came on. "We're on Lighthouse Lane headed toward the beach! Someone is trying to run us off the road!"

Tires squealed as Charles took the curve. Her seat belt cut into her shoulder. From the side mirror she could see the car following behind.

And then they were on a straighter part of the road.

With another curve just ahead.

From a side road, Demi could see flashing blue lights.

Brakes squealed from behind them and she saw the car backing off. It did a quick three-point turn then sped back the way they'd just come.

Charles slowed the truck. Sweat dripped from his forehead and his face had lost color, as he pulled to the side of the road and stopped.

From the back, Demi heard a giggle. She turned

to see Brianne gripping the front of her car seat. "Do it again, Daddy."

Aaron's eyes were wide, but he'd stopped crying. When he saw Brianne smiling, he chuckled.

Charles let out a breath and leaned his forehead on the steering wheel.

Demi swallowed hard. "You did a good job, Charles."

"Thanks." He paused. "You okay?"

"Yes. We're all okay."

A Fitzgerald Bay cruiser pulled up beside them. Charles rolled down his window to greet his sister Keira who exited her vehicle, walked to the window and demanded, "What happened? I saw that guy trying to run you off the road." Her anger with the man was a visible thing. "He could have killed you!" She looked in the backseat and paled. "And the kids are with you."

"We were on the way to the beach. He kind of came out of nowhere." Charles shook his head. "Did you get a plate?"

"A partial. He went flying past me. By the time I turned around, he'd disappeared. I called it in for someone to see if they could chase him down so I could make sure you all were okay."

Charles swallowed. "Someone really has it in for me, don't they?"

"Unfortunately, it looks like it, yeah." She pursed

her lips. "Who was Olivia so close to that her death would drive someone to want to hurt you, to get revenge?"

Charles shrugged. "I have no idea. She didn't talk about her life that much. I did a background check and she was clean. She took care of the kids and pretty much kept to herself so I'm not sure who she was close to."

"What about her cousin, Meghan?" Keira asked.

Charles gave a slow nod. "She was really upset about Olivia's death, but I can't see her coming after me like this."

Keira shrugged. "You never know. I'll make a note for Owen and Ryan to check her out." On a small flip-top notebook, she wrote something then slid it back into her front pocket. "Be careful, Charles. It looks like someone isn't very happy with you."

After consulting with Keira, Charles and Demi decided not to let the incident ruin their day.

And while Demi couldn't say she was relaxed, at least the person who had nearly run them off the road was gone for now.

But a shiver ran through her as the thought occurred to her that he would be back. Somehow, deep in her gut, she felt that it wasn't over. When they'd decided to keep their appointment with the beach, Keira promised to drive past the area often. "If whoever tried to run you off the road is watching, he'll see the cruiser keeping an eye on you."

"I don't know if that's necessary, Keira."

She shrugged. "I don't, either, but it can't hurt."

"Guess not." Charles looked at Demi and she offered him a reassuring smile.

Now at the beach, Demi climbed from the truck and while Charles unbuckled Brianne, she went ahead and released Aaron from his car seat.

Then the four of them headed down the pier. Brianne seemed to have forgotten about her demand for ice cream since the incident with the car.

Charles limped slightly and again, Demi wondered what happened. Before she could be nosy again, his brows pulled tight into a frown as he gazed at the cliffs and rocks under the lighthouse.

Wondering at the expression, Demi looked where he did. The white lighthouse with the red roof matched the building next to it. Charles's home. It sat at the top of a cliff overlooking the ocean. Just yesterday, she'd stood at the window and stared at the view. She'd been in awe of such beauty. "What a great place to raise kids."

"I think so." He shot her another smile, but it didn't reach his eyes and the frown between his brows seemed even more pronounced. "The path to the beach is this way. Be careful, there are a lot of rocks."

Demi held on to Aaron and followed Charles,

noticing that he carried a picnic basket in one hand while holding tight to Brianne's small hand.

Once on the beach, Charles opened the large basket, pulled out two towels and handed one to Demi. "I decided not to bring the chairs. We can use these. We won't stay very long. I'll have to get the twins back to the house for their nap."

The wind whipped her ponytail around her face and tugged at the towels. Demi followed his example and planted herself on one. He'd placed them close together so that her shoulder nearly touched his.

As her gaze scanned the area, she caught sight of the cruiser sitting at the top of the rock. Keira stood looking down at them. Peace settled on Demi's shoulders for the first time since finding the note this morning.

His musky cologne wafted to her and she inhaled, deciding she could get used to that smell. "It's chilly for May, isn't it?"

"Chilly and windy."

Brianne and Aaron each grabbed a bucket and shovel from the basket. "Daddy, you help me?" Brianne asked. "I want a castle for a princess."

Charles shook his head. "In a minute, Bri. I want to talk to Ms. Demi, okay?"

Brianne cocked her head and turned her shy smile on Demi. "You come help me?"

She would have been happy to dig in the sand

with the little ones, but took her cue from Charles. "Why don't you get started and I'll help you in a few minutes."

"Okay." Brianne joined her brother and the two started digging and flinging the sand.

Demi watched the little ones as she waited for Charles to say something. When he remained silent, she turned to look at him. His eyes were on his children, but even only knowing him such a short time, she could tell his thoughts were elsewhere. "What are you thinking?"

He blinked. "Nothing much."

She didn't believe it, but didn't feel it was her place to push him. The hair on the back of her neck lifted and she shifted. Uneasiness shivered through her and she looked toward the cliffs again. That feeling of being watched just wouldn't leave her.

Keira was still there, now perched on the hood of her cruiser, talking on the phone. Her presence offered comfort. So where was Demi's edginess coming from? Someone after *her?* Or were these incidents all related to Charles, and she was just caught in the middle?

The latter, more likely. That's what everyone seemed to think with the incident at his house or the one on the road just now. But what about the break-in at her apartment?

Something just wasn't right, but Demi couldn't

figure out exactly what it was that was making her so uneasy.

If someone was watching Charles right now, he didn't seem to notice.

He handed her a sandwich, breaking her train of thought. "Do you like ham and cheese?"

"Love it. Thanks." She unwrapped it and took a bite as she watched the kids. Even though she had her eyes on the children, she was extremely aware of the man beside her—and the fact that her back was exposed to a number of hiding places in the rocks behind her.

"This is the first time we've been down here this year," he said suddenly.

His quiet words surprised her. She heard the strain behind them. "Really? Why?"

He turned his gaze to her. "Because of what happened to Olivia, of course."

"Oh." She looked around again. "Is this where it happened?"

"Not exactly, but pretty close. She fell—or was pushed—over the cliffs. She was found down there on the rocks below our house and the lighthouse. They found a rock with blood on it and are running tests to see if they can find any DNA on it. We're waiting for those tests to come back."

"I'm sorry you're having such a rough time."

His eyes softened and he lifted a hand as though

to reach out to her. Then must have decided against it as he snagged a bottle of water. "Thanks."

Demi wondered if now would be good time to say something about the note in her coffee can. Opening her mouth to do that, she was interrupted by Charles's phone ringing. "Just a sec." He found the device and said, "Hello?" She watched him listen. Then he said, "That's fine, we're not staying much longer anyway."

He hung up and told her, "Keira needs to leave in a few minutes." His lips quirked in a small smile. "She said she'd feel better if we'd leave when she did."

"We can if you like."

"Not yet. The children are loving this." His gaze met hers. "And so am I."

Demi flushed as she caught his unspoken message. She decided to change the subject. "So what's your family like?"

His smile widened. She hadn't fooled him one bit. "You've already met a few of them. Fiona, your landlady, is my sister, and Victoria, who owns the Sugar Plum Café, is my sister-in-law-to-be. Probably one day soon. She's engaged to Owen, a detective. The rest of the crew are also with the Fitzgerald Bay Police Department as you found out last night. My mother died a few years ago and Dad's the chief of police and running for mayor against the oh-so-subtle Burke Hennessy. My granddad, Ian Fitzgerald, is the current mayor, and is stepping down. I have three brothers and two sisters."

Demi sighed. "I'm envious. I have no idea if I have any family anywhere." She looked at the cliffs where Olivia died. Clouds moved in and hovered, obscuring the sun. Demi shivered.

"Are you cold?"

"A bit."

"Daddy! Come play!" Brianne insisted.

Charles quirked another smile at her. "I guess we can warm up while we help them dig that hole to China." He looked up as Keira's cruiser pulled away. "Then I guess we'd better head home and let two little ones get some shut-eye."

Demi grabbed a shovel and sank beside Aaron. He grinned up at her and said, "Dig."

"Say please, Aaron," Charles reminded his son.

"Puleeeeeze," Aaron said with a grin.

But even as she sank the shovel into the soft sand, she couldn't help watching behind her. Talking with Charles and spending time with his family had been a wonderful diversion from her less-than-pleasant thoughts. However, the feeling of being watched never fully left her.

The cliffs were steep, the rocks sharp and dangerous. She felt a deep pang of sympathy for the woman who'd died there. Turning, she concentrated on digging.

The sound of a low growl snapped up her head. A

dog stood on the rocks watching them. "Charles?" she whispered.

He turned and she heard his indrawn breath.

"It's a German shepherd." He kept his voice low and she heard the tension running through it.

"He—or she—doesn't look very friendly." Demi gripped the toy shovel as though she would be able to use it as a weapon. Slowly, her eyes never leaving the dog, she moved between it and the children.

The animal bared its teeth once more and Charles reached for a piece of driftwood. He flung it toward the dog with a harsh, "Get!"

The dog flinched, tucked her tail and ran off.

Demi let out her breath in a huff as she wilted on the sand. "I wonder if she has puppies around here."

"You're amazing."

"What?" Demi gaped at him. Why would he say that?

He nodded, his eyes serious and intense. "Your first instinct was to protect the children with no thought of yourself. I've never met…I mean other than family…I don't know of anyone that would have done that."

"Daddy, play!" Brianne called, oblivious to the danger she could have just been in. Charles gazed into her eyes a moment longer then turned to pay attention to his daughter.

Speechless and surprised at his praise, Demi still shivered at the feeling of trepidation that swept over her. Especially when she thought about that note in the coffee can.

She swallowed hard and hoped that by being vigilant and watchful, she wouldn't be the next victim the cliffs would claim.

SIX

Sunday morning, Demi woke early, tossed and turned until she heaved a sigh of frustration. Climbing from the bed, she decided to head to the beach for a walk. She'd so enjoyed the time with Charles and the kids yesterday that she wanted to feel the wind in her face and the sand beneath her feet before she had to get ready for church.

Within minutes, she was out the door on the bike that Fiona had said she could use anytime. It was a long ride, but she didn't care. Being outside was chilly, but exhilarating. Already she felt lighter, like her burdens were sliding from her shoulders.

At the end of the wooden boardwalk that led to the beach, she slipped off her sandals and dug her toes into the cool sand.

For a moment she just stood there, watching the waves crash against the shore.

To her left, she saw another person walking her way. Squinting, pushing up her glasses as though that would help bring the individual into focus, she watched.

A man with a gray hoodie.

Spinning on the sand, she headed back the way she'd come. Who was he? Had he somehow followed her?

Demi shivered and shot a glance over her shoulder. The man was closing in.

She considered turning around and confronting him, but the thought of Olivia Henry, and the fact that her murderer still roamed free, spurred her faster toward the walkway.

True, the man could be harmless.

Or, he could have a weapon.

No sense in finding out the hard way.

She hurried along, but couldn't help one more glance over her shoulder.

The man had stopped following and just stood there watching her walk away.

She wished she could get a good look at his face, but with the hood pulled up and low, it was impossible. However, she thought she saw him lift his hand in a small wave.

Demi gulped and continued her hurried pace along the walkway that would lead her to her bicycle. Another glance back told her that the man had started walking again, but at a leisurely pace, seeming in no hurry to catch up.

Would he come up to the walkway, as well?

No. Demi adjusted her glasses a little higher on her nose. He looked like he was leaving. She watched him turn and head back down the beach. Her pulse slowed slightly.

But she desperately wanted to know who he was. If he was the one who'd broken into her apartment and put the message in her coffee can, she wanted to know why.

But she'd never seen him anywhere other than the alley behind The Reading Nook and now. If it was even the same person.

Grasping the handlebars, she swung her leg over the bike and placed her foot on the pedal.

Only now she felt a shiver go through her at the idea of riding to her apartment all alone.

Safely back home, Demi dressed for church. Shoving aside the creepy encounter with the stranger on the beach, she allowed herself a small measure of joy. Yesterday she'd managed to put aside the note in her coffee can and just as she'd hoped, the day had been lovely—except for almost being run off the road and the dog scare on the beach.

However, she'd take what she could get at this point.

Spending time with Charles and the children had filled a void she hadn't been consciously aware of until she'd had to leave them and come home.

Worry bit at her. Would she feel this way if she had her memories intact? Or was she using them to make up for what she lacked in her life?

Unsure of the answer, she decided there was nothing she could do about it right now.

As she pulled the brush through her hair one last time, she gave herself a quick check in the mirror. The flower-print dress made her feel pretty and feminine and she wondered what Charles would think. She flushed and turned from the mirror. She didn't bother trying to tell herself she shouldn't care what Charles thought. She was attracted to the man and that was that.

And he'd invited her to church. She'd agreed and told him that she would meet him there. When he'd offered to pick her up, she'd hesitated then said no. She'd confused him, she could tell, but with all the rumors flying around about Charles, she didn't want to add fuel to the fire by being seen walking into church with him after having already spent yesterday with him.

She had a feeling she was only prolonging the moment, though. Word was already out that Charles had a new nanny and she figured the wagging tongues were going triple time. And if she sat with him in church this morning…she might as well have let him come get her.

But she couldn't concern herself with that. Or

listen to gossip. She was going to go to church and enjoy it.

She'd passed the Fitzgerald Bay Community Church located just off Main Street during her explorations of the town, and had given some thought to stepping inside, wondering if she would find God there.

Now was the time to find out.

"Demi? You ready?"

Fiona had promised to stop by and walk with her to church. Turning from the window, Demi determined to put her fears to rest and enjoy the day.

She crossed the room and opened the door to see Fiona dressed in a khaki skirt and a light pink pullover summer sweater.

"Good morning. Come on in while I get my purse." Demi grabbed it from the chair.

"Sean and Hunter left a bit early so they could have their 'man breakfast.'" Fiona laughed. "No girls allowed."

Together, she and Fiona descended the stairs. "That's so sweet. Hunter is like a father to Sean, isn't he?"

"Yes, after my first husband, Jimmy, died, I was crushed, but—" a real smile spread across her face "—Hunter has been an answer to prayer. He loves Sean like he's his own. And Sean returns the affection. God's been good to us."

"Even with all the crazy stuff going on?" She'd

heard about the fire at the bookstore and the arsonist who'd been caught just before Demi's arrival in town.

Fiona smiled. "Even then."

Outside, they started the short walk to the church and Demi couldn't help glancing around, and back over her shoulder.

"Are you okay?" Fiona asked.

Demi jumped. "Oh. Yes, I'm fine. I'm sorry, I guess I'm just a bit skittish."

"Well, who can blame you after what happened at Charles's house Friday night? And then to come home and think someone had been in your apartment? I'd be skittish, too." She paused. "So you really think someone was there?"

Demi frowned. "Yes, I do. I just don't know why."

Fiona gave her a sympathetic pat on the arm and frowned. "I have someone coming today to reinforce the locks."

"Might not be a bad idea." In fact Demi thought it was a very good idea.

And then they were at the church. It was a lovely white-steepled structure with old-world charm. Demi hoped she would be able to find some peace inside.

Fiona led the way and Demi followed her down the aisle, watching as the woman spoke to nearly everyone there. She introduced Demi as a friend and her new tenant.

And then the man who'd been so snarly the other day, Burke Hennessy, walked up and gave her a haughty smirk. "You don't have much of a self-preservation instinct, do you?"

"What do you mean?"

Burke's voice carried through the chattering crowd. "I'm just trying to give you some advice, dear. Getting mixed up with the Fitzgerald family isn't the smartest move in the playbook. Charles is a murderer. His family's position at the police department is the only reason he's not behind bars."

Demi blinked at the man's audacity.

"Burke, enough," the pretty blonde at his side hissed. The crowd immediately around them had quieted and now watched the interaction play out.

"It'll never be enough, Christina," Burke continued. "Fitzgerald Bay hasn't had a murder in over forty years and—"

Fiona broke in, "Burke, not everyone believes the vicious rumors being spread about my brother. Leave Demi and Charles alone."

Fiona pulled Demi away from the man still watching, his eyes burning holes into the back of her. Demi shivered at the underlying menace in the man's voice.

By the time they walked to the middle of the church, Demi's mind spun with names and faces and Burke Hennessy's warning. Was he right? Was she being stupid to get involved with a man under the shadow of a murder investigation?

Her gaze landed on Charles—and the rest of his family.

His huge family, surrounding him, offered a buffer against the cold self-righteousness of members who didn't believe a man suspected of murder should be in a house of worship. But she was glad to see others treated Charles well, slapping him on the back and shaking his hand. Apparently they'd missed the exchange with Burke.

All eyes seemed to land on her at the same time and panic hit her. What if the Fitzgeralds didn't like her? Up to this point, the only time she'd had any real contact with his family was when she'd called 9-1-1 and they'd all shown up at Charles's house.

What if they thought she was crazy because of the amnesia? What if they didn't think she was good enough to take care of the twins? What if—

Charles lifted his head and caught her eyes. Pushing his way out of the circle around him, he held out a hand. "Good morning, Demi. Let me introduce you to the members of the family you haven't met yet."

Once again, Demi took in the names she knew she'd never remember, but was grateful no one seemed to find it strange that Charles had invited her. In fact everyone welcomed her with open arms.

Then the music started and Demi slipped into the

pew beside Charles. She was glad she'd come, but she couldn't help glancing around the congregation.

She continued to scan the crowd, eyes probing, looking for any hint of recognition. But she saw nothing that triggered her internal alarm. She thought of the person on the beach. And then the one who'd tried to get into the building via the back door. Was it the same man?

She wasn't sure. All she knew was that the hairs on the back of her neck stood up. And somehow, she knew someone was here in this church…watching her.

Charles glanced at the woman beside him as his mind spun with ideas to help her. He was having a hard time staying focused on the sermon. A problem he had developed shortly after Kathleen left him. If it wasn't for the children, he wasn't sure he'd even bother to attend. Might as well figure out a way to help Demi in the meantime.

She seemed so fragile, so needy and yet he'd seen strength in her when her first instinct had been to protect the children from the dog—or protect him from whatever was in her closet.

Those were things he wasn't likely to forget any time soon.

And the children had been asking about her this morning as he got them ready for church. They'd already fallen in love with their new nanny. Charles knew that if she decided to quit because of all the things that were happening to her—things that were happening because she was involved with him and his family—the children would be heartbroken.

A little voice in the back of his head said he would be, too.

Then he'd seen Burke say something to her at the start of the service and figured it wasn't good. She'd looked spooked, then worried, but her expression had smoothed as the music had started.

Whatever had been bothering her at the beginning of the service seemed to slide from her shoulders and her mood lightened.

Was she a believer?

He made a mental note to ask her. Then scoffed at himself. She had amnesia. How would she know?

Charles leaned back and relaxed, glad to be in the company of his family. They shielded him from the dark looks the good people of Fitzgerald Bay shot him even in the church.

Movement from behind the pulpit grabbed his attention. Long heavy blue velvet curtains hung behind the pastor. One fluttered.

Then stopped.

Charles frowned as he watched for more movement. He looked for the air conditioning vent, but didn't see one.

Nothing else happened over the next several minutes and he started to relax.

When the congregation erupted in laughter, Charles jerked. He'd been so preoccupied with the movement of the curtains, he'd missed the joke.

He tuned back in.

Pastor Larch said, "And now we have a video that will show you a little bit of what our young people will be doing on their mission trip to the mountains of North Carolina."

The lights dimmed.

The curtains parted and the music started.

As the curtains pulled apart, Charles gaped at the words that were revealed on the lighted screen.

YOU DON'T BELONG HERE.

Beside him, Demi jerked and gasped.

The congregation muttered and pointed.

Aiden Fitzgerald popped to his feet as did Ryan, Owen and Keira. "Turn the lights back on!" Aiden shouted.

The sanctuary lit up.

Aiden, followed by several other members of the Fitzgerald Bay Police Department and leaders of the church, strode to the screen.

Charles joined them, heart thudding, listening to their speculation even as he studied the message.

Was it meant for him?

"Don't touch anything," he heard his father order.

Keira said, "Everyone back up, please. Can you all please return to your seats?"

But all Charles could do was stare. And it became very real to him that there were people in this town who not only thought he was a murderer, but hated him. Hated him enough to attack him in his own church. Hated him enough to vandalize his home and terrorize his family.

Anger bubbled just beneath the surface and he turned. He'd get his kids and get out. Turning, he saw Demi staring at the words, her face pale, her eyes wide. Scared.

His gut clenched. Would she now tell him that she no longer wanted anything to do with him? With his children?

The thought stabbed him in the heart.

"Demi?"

She turned her gaze on him, shook her head and walked toward the back of the church.

Ryan Fitzgerald, Deputy Chief of Police, came to stand beside him. "You think this was because of you, don't you?"

"Don't you?" Charles gritted out.

The uncertainty that flashed across Ryan's face was answer enough. Then Ryan shrugged. "Probably, but I wouldn't let it get to me. You know how people are, bro. Let it roll off your back."

"Not everyone feels that way, Charles," Pastor

Larch said from his left. Charles turned to see the compassionate gaze of the man. "Don't let this run you off. You belong here just as much as the person who left that message."

"Thank you, Pastor, but I think it's best if I just leave for now." He appreciated the man's reassurance, but the only thing he was interested in was getting his children and finding Demi.

Charles touched Fiona's arm to get her attention in the chaos. "Will you get the twins? I need to take care of something."

Concern reflected in her gaze, but instead of questioning him, she nodded. "Sure. We're going to Dad's for lunch." She looked again at the front of the church where the message still blazed. "At least we were."

"I'll be back in a minute."

He ran after Demi.

He means me, she thought. It was the same message as the one in the coffee can. *I don't belong here. He's right.* But how did he know that? And why make such a public display of it? To send her running?

Did she belong anywhere? To anyone?

Sobs crowded her throat as she made her way down the front steps of the church. She'd tried so hard to be brave, to believe the amnesia would go away and her memory would return.

But it hadn't.

Tears slipped down her cheeks and she ignored them.

Anger, self-pity and fear all swirled inside her. Why had she even bothered coming to church? Did she somehow think that by doing so she could make God happy and He would miraculously restore her memory?

Maybe.

Her sandaled feet slapped the sidewalk as she hurried toward her apartment. She would have to use the phone in The Reading Nook to call Charles and—

Charles.

She stumbled to a halt.

And felt a heavy hand land on her arm.

Gasping, she spun and saw Charles.

"You s-scared me to death," she stuttered.

His grim mouth tightened even more. "I know. I seem to have that effect on most of the townspeople these days."

"I'm sorry."

His brows drew even closer together as he frowned. "What do you mean? Sorry for what? I'm the one who needs to apologize to you."

That stopped her. Drawing in a deep breath, she said, "Oh. Why?"

"I suppose after that little surprise in the church,

you've rethought your decision to work as the children's nanny?"

"What?" she blurted out. "No! I figured you wouldn't want me anymore after...wait a minute. You think that message was for you?"

"Well, of course, who else..." Realization dawned on him. "And you think it was for you." His frown lightened a fraction. "But why?" When she didn't answer right away, he said, "I think we need to talk."

She glanced behind him. "Where are the children?"

"With Fiona." His gentle hand swiped the tears from her cheeks leaving a heated trail behind.

She flushed but hoped he would contribute that to the emotion of the moment. "Who would do such a thing?" she whispered.

"I don't know. I thought I saw the curtain moving before the lights went low, but I didn't think much about it." He swallowed hard. Looked away then back at her. "I have a confession to make."

"What?" Should she be worried?

But his eyes were kind. Gentle. And sad. He lifted his shoulders in a slight shrug. "I haven't been to church in a while. I got tired of the stares, the accusing looks, the mamas hiding their children when I passed by." He blew out a breath. "But today, I wanted to be there—" He met her eyes. "With you." He gave a wry smile. "I fought in Iraq, toe-to-toe most days with some pretty harsh guys. But going to church, facing those people intimidated me." Now he looked away. "I felt weak. And don't ask me to explain this, but going to church today, knowing you were coming, knowing there was one person besides my family who believed in me..." He pulled in a deep breath. "That made me feel strong."

"Oh, Charles." She stepped forward and wrapped her arms around his waist and offered him a hug right there on Main Street. In front of God and anyone else who cared to see. When she pulled away, the surprise in his eyes made her flush. "I'm sorry."

"Don't be." His voice was husky as though holding back some deep emotion. "I needed that."

"There you are."

They jumped as one as the voice echoed across the street. Demi turned to see Aiden Fitzgerald bearing down on them, one brow raised. He didn't say anything about the embrace he just witnessed. "We've got that mess taken care of back there. Now, can we put all this unpleasantness behind us and go eat? I'm starved." His father eyed Charles who still had a hand on her upper arm. "You're coming for lunch, right?"

"Sure, Dad, wouldn't miss it." Demi could hear the forced cheerfulness. "Who's cooking?"

"Keira and Fiona threw something together last night. Just need to heat it up."

Charles glanced at Demi.

"Demi's welcome, too," his father said.

"Thanks." He looked at her. "Will you join us?"

"I'm…um…" Uncertainty filled her. She should probably say no. But she wanted to go. "Yes, I'd love that, thank you."

"Great. You can ride with me and the kids."

"I just need to get my purse. I'm afraid I ran off without it." She ignored the embarrassed flush she felt climbing her cheeks.

"You get your purse. I'll get the kids from Fiona and meet you at the truck."

Demi nodded, excited at the prospect of spending more time with Charles and his family. And yet that excitement was tempered by the knowledge that while Charles thought that message was for him, she felt quite sure he was wrong.

Although she was unable to explain the reasons behind it.

SEVEN

"Thanks for inviting her, Dad."

"No problem. She's a pretty girl."

Charles felt a flush at the back of his neck. "Don't go there, Dad. Lunch would be a great way for her to get to know the family. I mean she is the kids' nanny, so everyone should get to know her. And she should get to know them. I mean—"

His father gave a hearty chuckle and slapped Charles on the back. "You can stop that painful explanation any time now."

In spite of the morning's incident, Charles found a grin. "Right. I'm just going to get the kids from Fiona."

"Do you mind if I walk with you?"

"Sure, I never turn down an extra pair of hands."

As they walked, his father said, "I know you're anxious to hear about the DNA test results."

"I am."

"I called the lab yesterday and they said it would

probably be another few days to a week. We should know something soon."

Charles's jaw clamped tight. He knew his family was doing everything they could to clear his name. And he knew that getting DNA results back in a reasonable amount of time was next to impossible. So he would wait. Maybe not patiently, but he would wait.

They arrived at the nursery to find Fiona gathering Brianne and Aaron. When Brianne saw her father, she squealed and opened her arms to him. He scooped her up, smelling her little-girl scent and thanking God for blessing his life with the two little ones.

"Daddy, I'm hungry. Want some ice cream," Brianne said.

"Me, too," Aaron agreed.

"Let's go eat some lunch first," Charles said. "Then we'll talk about ice cream. You have to eat veggies."

"No veggies." Brianne frowned. "No, no, no."

"Yes, veggies. Yes, yes, yes."

His father carried Aaron while Charles continued his dialogue with Brianne. At the car, he found Demi waiting, her smile welcoming, but the strain of the morning still stamped on her face. His father handed Aaron over to her and she helped him load the kids into their car seats.

His dad said, "See you at the house," then walked toward his own car.

As a result of Demi's presence, Charles couldn't help notice that the cloud of loneliness that Kathleen's desertion had caused seemed to lift. He watched Demi tickle Aaron under his chin and laugh. Aaron laughed back and tried to copy Demi by wiggling his little fingers under her chin.

Longing hit him. Hard. He wanted someone in his life. Someone who loved him, loved his kids. Someone like Demi.

As he climbed behind the wheel, he scoffed at himself. Someone like Demi? He'd known the woman all of a week and it made him nervous that he was thinking long-term about her because he wasn't sure he could trust his instincts anymore. They'd certainly been wrong about Kathleen. Could he trust them about Demi?

And what about the person that seemed determined to keep flinging the blame for Olivia's murder in his face? And the fact that most people in town considered him a suspect? He looked in the rearview mirror at his children, then over at Demi.

His heart shuddered at the thought of something happening to them. In addition to keeping them all safe and clearing his name, he wanted to help Demi figure out who she was. But how?

Unable to come up with a satisfying answer, he thought about the Glock he had locked in his safe at home. Might be a good time to start carrying it again. It would be one step toward keeping everyone safe.

"Are you all right?"

Charles jerked. Demi looked at him, her wide green eyes waiting for his answer.

"Yes," he smiled. "Just thinking."

"About what?"

"A lot of things. But one thing was about trying to figure out a way to help you."

Interest brightened her face. "Like how?"

"Just an idea I've got brewing in the back of my mind. Let me put it to my brother Owen and see what he thinks. If he decides it has merit, I'll fill you in."

She frowned, but didn't question him as she settled back into the seat. The drive to his father's house didn't take long.

Inside, Victoria's daughter, Paige, volunteered to entertain the children in the playroom. Charles let her, watched Keira take Demi under her wing and then headed off to the den to find Owen talking with Ryan and Hunter.

Owen's large frame hogged one end of the couch. Charles got his attention and waved him over. Curiosity etched on his features, Owen followed Charles into the hall. "What's up?"

"I want to help Demi try to figure out who she is."

Owen knew about the amnesia. Word had spread

quickly that Charles had hired a woman with no memory. "What do you have in mind?"

"Demi said the police posted her picture in the papers and on the news for several days after she woke up, but no one came to identify her."

"Could be the wrong part of the country. Could be she doesn't have anyone."

Charles frowned. "That's a sad thought."

"Yeah." Owen glanced toward the den. "I know if one of us disappeared, Dad would stop at nothing to find us."

Charles knew that for a fact. "So what do you think about putting her picture back up on the news? See if we get a response?"

Owen shrugged. "Sure, we can do it." He pulled his phone from his pocket. "You got a picture of her?"

Charles grabbed his own phone. "I will in a minute."

"I'll let Deborah know it's coming." Deborah was the dispatcher. She'd see the picture was handled appropriately.

Charles went in search of Demi and found her in the dining room placing a huge bowl of mashed potatoes in the center of the table. Even growing up in this family, he was still amazed at the amount of food they put away whenever they got together.

She smiled when she saw him. He waved her over. "I need a picture of you."

Her right brow lifted. "Okay. What for?"

"We're going to put your picture back out there on the news one more time and see if anyone steps forward."

Grief flashed for a brief moment before she lifted her chin. "We already tried that. In the city where I was attacked. Springfield, Massachusetts. About a hundred miles west of here." She shrugged and swallowed. "I don't think there is anyone."

Charles felt his heart break for her. He placed his hands on her shoulders and said, "Demi, no one is completely alone in the world. Even if someone is the last surviving member of her family, there are still friends, coworkers, *someone* who would notice if she were missing."

"But no one did," she whispered. "That's what I'm saying."

"Then the right person didn't see the picture," he insisted.

"Are you always this stubborn?"

"Always," Owen said from behind him.

She glanced between the brothers and then shrugged. "Okay, if you want to try."

Charles snapped the picture and sent it to Owen's phone so that it got displayed on the six o'clock news that night.

"Owen," Victoria interrupted, holding out her phone. "Trevor Billings is on the phone. Wants to know if you can fill in and pitch the upcoming softball game. It's the special fundraiser game for the children's hospital and Kyle can't be there."

Charles watched his brother roll his eyes and explain to a confused Demi, "Trevor is the team's manager. He recruits us from church. Kyle is the regular pitcher. I pitched one game for him last season and now they're determined to get me on that team full-time. I told them I didn't have time for that right now. That I couldn't commit."

Victoria's gaze softened as she looked at her fiancé and Charles felt a pang hit him. Would he ever see that look in a woman's eyes again? He stole a glance at Demi and saw her watching them, a longing also written on her face.

Victoria said, "You need to take some time for you, Owen. You're going to burn out if you don't have a little fun. You can't spend every single minute working." Then she flushed and looked at Charles. "No offense, Charles."

He smiled. "None taken. In fact I agree with you. It's for a great cause." He said to Owen, "Go on, they need you. We may even bring the kids and cheer you on."

After another brief hesitation, Owen sighed and nodded his consent, but Charles thought he could see a gleam of anticipation in his brother's eyes.

Victoria smiled. "Great. I'll tell him that you'll be there."

Hours later, as Charles took Demi home, he asked her, "So, did we scare you off?"

She laughed. "No. You have a wonderful family."

"Thanks. I think so. Most of the time."

"And you didn't have to feed me supper. I could have come home long before now."

He frowned. "I'm sorry, I should have thought you might have something to do or things to take care of... I didn't... I mean... Did you want to leave?"

Another laugh escaped her and he decided that he could listen to that sound all day.

"No. And I didn't have anything to do. It was a lovely way to spend the day. Thank you."

Relief filled him. "Good. So, I'll see you tomorrow?"

"Eight o'clock sharp."

"Great. I have a nine o'clock appointment."

"I'll be there."

"I'll let you know if there's any calls about your picture on the news."

"Okay. Thanks."

As she started to climb out of the car, he couldn't stop himself from snagging her hand.

Startled, her eyes met his and he said, "Thank you for coming today. I'm sorry about the mess at the church."

She shrugged. "It wasn't your fault. And I enjoyed the time with your family."

Her hand felt soft, yet strong. And he wasn't ready to let go yet. But he did because he had to. He needed to keep their relationship more professional than personal. At least right now. He swallowed hard and wondered how he was going to be able to do that when everything in him wanted to get to know her better—and his reason had nothing to do with business. "I'll see you in the morning."

Demi bit her lip as she let herself into the apartment even as she wondered about the look that had been in Charles's eyes when he'd said goodbye. A longing.

And a distance.

Weird.

Her heart trembled at the thought of her face being on the news once again. If a silent phone followed the broadcast, she would be heartbroken.

So, the only way to avoid that was to refuse to get her hopes up. But she appreciated Charles's desire to help.

Speaking of help…

Her eyes went to the kitchen cabinet. She hadn't told him about the note. Each time she'd thought about it, there hadn't been a chance to bring it up without another member of the family overhearing.

And in the truck, she'd simply wimped out. She didn't want to hurt him. Telling him about the note would be just another arrow in his already aching heart. He would feel guilty. Possibly even tell her that she needed to find another job.

She shuddered. She didn't want to find another job and she didn't want Charles worrying that he was putting her in any kind of danger.

So, she'd keep her mouth shut.

For now.

As Chloe wrapped a warm welcome around Demi's ankles, she felt her tense shoulders relax. She hadn't realized she'd been worried about coming home.

Facing her apartment all alone.

At least the door had definitely been locked this time, but she still worried.

Worry. Fear. Anxiety. Emotions she had become intimately familiar with over the past few weeks.

But excitement lingered, too. She had a job. True, she had no car and no driver's license, and it was a fifteen-minute walk to and from Charles's house, but that was no big deal.

As she puttered and cleaned a little, getting ready to relax for the rest of the evening—or at least try to if she could keep her gaze from straying to the cabinet that held the coffee canister—she realized she'd finished the last book she'd borrowed from

The Reading Nook. Since she had no television, books had been her sole entertainment in the evenings.

She supposed she could just go to bed, but it was only eight-thirty and she was still wound up from the excitement of the day. Charles had been so attentive, his family kind and welcoming. And she almost wished she hadn't gone.

Being around the Fitzgeralds, watching their interactions, listening to their teasing, their good-natured arguing, had spiked a longing in her that nearly split her in two. What would it be like to be a part of a family like that? To know that someone would miss her immediately if she suddenly wasn't there?

Tears formed and she blinked them back.

She looked at Chloe who sat on the floor cleaning a paw. "I definitely needed a book to read."

Chloe looked up at Demi's words then went back to her business.

Since Fiona had told Demi to help herself anytime she found herself wanting something to read, Demi decided to take her up on that offer.

Making her way downstairs, she was grateful Fiona didn't bother to lock the door leading from the apartment stairs to the bookstore area. She supposed Fiona felt that locking the outer doors was enough security.

The dark interior made her shiver. But she knew exactly which book she wanted.

The Bible.

Fiona had a whole shelf of Bibles in every translation available. As Demi made her way through the store, she thought she saw a flash of light toward the back. She frowned and couldn't help the tremor of fear that shot through her.

It surprised her so much, she nearly stumbled. The darkness pressed in on her, suffocating her. Another flash of light near the window, then nothing.

More darkness. She couldn't handle the darkness. Her breathing quickened as she shoved down the fear that came from nowhere.

Why am I so afraid?

Gasping, she flew to the wall that held the light switch and flipped it.

Nothing happened.

She flipped it again. Down, then up.

Her stomach quivered and the images flared up again. The heavy fist, a flash of agonizing pain in her head. Angry words.

"Stop." She flinched at the harsh word then realized it had come from her. "Stop," she whispered.

The images faded, but the lights still didn't work.

Why not? They worked fine in her apartment.

A sliding scrape to her right froze her, heart pounding, blood rushing.

Was someone in the store?

After all that had happened since she'd arrived in Fitzgerald Bay, every nerve jumped into hyper-awareness. Was that someone breathing? Should she call out? Warn the person she was there?

No, she had a feeling the person knew she was there. And she was right where he wanted her.

EIGHT

Charles tucked the twins into bed and kissed them each good-night at least five times. He was exhausted. Thank goodness he'd had his family helping him today or he wouldn't have been able to function.

As much as he loved his children, they wore him out. Being a single father had not been the plan. But that's the way things had worked out and while he wished his marriage hadn't ended the way it had, he was grateful for the two beautiful children that had come from it.

He walked to the window and looked out. A police cruiser sat in plain view. Charles felt his jaw tighten. While thankful for the extra pair of eyes, he was frustrated at the necessity for it.

His right hand reached up to touch the weapon in the shoulder holster. It felt right. Comforting. Even as the need for it brought to mind the memories of his time in Iraq. A time he'd rather forget.

Now Olivia's death, the spray paint on his garage,

the incident at church had him jumping at shadows and looking over his shoulder. Just like back in Iraq, he was now in a constant adrenaline rush.

He closed his eyes and did his best to concentrate on the good in his life.

As a result, he found himself looking forward to work tomorrow for the first time since Olivia's death and felt certain that had something to do with the fact that Demi's faith in him was salve to his wounded soul.

In addition to that, he hoped that with Demi's agreeing to be the children's nanny, people would stop looking at him like he was monster.

Last week at the office had been a little better.

Maybe this week he would continue to see an improvement.

Since Olivia's death, it had been only the sickest who'd been willing to see him. And some long-time patients who didn't believe the drivel they'd seen on the television and read in the newspaper. But those were few and far between. Especially with Burke spouting his nonsense.

Back on the positive side, he couldn't help the little leap his heart gave at the thought that he would see Demi in the morning for a brief time before he had to take off. Maybe they would even have a chance to share a cup of coffee together. He settled into the recliner to watch the end of the movie he'd DVR'd the night before.

Just as he picked up the remote, his phone buzzed.

He frowned when he saw the number was Owen's. Punching the talk button, he said, "Hello?"

"Just got a call from someone who said they thought they saw someone sneaking around Fiona's store. Do you know where she is?"

Charles's feet slammed to the floor. "No, did you try Hunter? Who made the call?"

"I don't know. Said they saw what looked like a flashlight bouncing around inside and thought it might be a prowler. And yes, I tried Hunter. He's not answering his phone and neither is Fiona."

"I'll meet you there." All of a sudden his fatigue was gone, replaced by racing adrenaline. Demi lived above that store. What if she went down there and ran into an intruder?

"No need, it might be nothing and I'll keep you updated."

"Mrs. Mulrooney can be here in five minutes. I'll be at the store in little more than ten."

He hung up and dialed his father's housekeeper. Charles explained his dilemma and she promised to come right over.

As soon as she stepped in the door, he said a hasty thanks and ran to his truck.

Demi clutched the phone as she waited in the dark, ears straining. She listened for the slightest sound, praying help would arrive soon. But how could it? The phone was dead.

She prayed that she was wrong, that she was just hearing things. That she was safe and no one was in the store with her.

A footstep to her right made her jerk.

Her heart tripled its erratic beat and she held her breath. She wasn't just hearing things. Just like she hadn't imagined the message in her coffee grounds.

She was on her own with no way to call for help. Her eyes darted in the dark, doing her best to ignore the desire to give in to the panic clawing at her.

In her mind's eye, she visualized the layout of the store. She was behind the counter where the phone was. To her left were the numerous bookcases, shelves filled with volumes.

A sitting area just beyond that.

Another footstep, closer this time, made her heart leap again.

Why wouldn't he say anything? What was he doing? Why did he want to frighten her?

"Who's there?" she called, her voice high, squeaky and scared. "What do you want?"

Now she heard his breathing, just beyond the counter. Why wouldn't he say something?

She had to move. Stay out of his reach until she could get out of the store. Right now, he stood between her and the door. If she tried to get back to the stairs leading to her apartment, she would be trapped by the locked door on one side and the intruder on the other.

Placing the phone on the floor, she took two steps to her left, gripped the edge of the counter and slipped around the side.

She caught motion to her right. The moon's light filtered through the blinds and now that her eyes had adjusted to the darkness, she could pick out shapes and shadows.

Which meant the intruder probably could, too.

Demi moved again. The shadow moved with her.

She ducked behind a bookcase and heard two more footsteps.

How was she going to get help?

Click.

What was that?

She didn't have time to dwell on that question as she could hear him coming closer.

Silently, she sidestepped around another bookcase, bumped her shin on a small table and sent it crashing to the floor.

It sounded like a sonic boom in the utter stillness of the store.

Breath hitching, Demi moved around the table to seek refuge behind another shelf.

She thought she heard a curse, muttering.

Then bright light filled the store through one of the windows and she saw the man standing next to one of the cushioned chairs. He froze like a deer caught in the headlights.

But she couldn't see his face.

He had his hoodie pulled up and she could only make out his profile.

Then he spun on his heel and headed for the back door of the store. Relief pounded through her. Anger followed swiftly behind. She was so tired of being a victim.

Should she try to stop him?

Her eyes darted, wondering how she could do it without getting hurt. By the time she decided she couldn't, he was gone anyway, out the back. The same way he'd probably come in.

But how had he gotten through a locked door?

Charles followed Owen as far as his brother would allow. "Stay here until I give the all clear, you understand?"

"Yeah, yeah, go."

Charles watched Owen place a hand on his weapon as he approached the front door to The Reading Nook. Everything in him itched to head in after Owen. Fighting in Iraq had prepared him to be in the thick of things. He'd willingly taken a backseat to the investigation into Olivia's death, letting his brothers do the job they'd been trained to do, but not knowing if Demi was all right was killing him.

He crept closer, watching as Owen drew his gun and stepped inside. A cold sweat broke over Charles as flashes from his days in the military, going house to house, searching for the wounded in the midst of the rebels and terrorists popped through his mind. Not knowing if you were going to be offered a drink or a bullet had kept his nerves on edge, his senses honed.

This was how he felt now. Would Demi be all right? Or not? Following a hunch, Charles did a one-eighty on his good leg and hoofed it around the side of the building.

Just in time to see a figure bolt through the back door of Fiona's bookstore.

"Hey! Stop!"

The person never paused, just kept pounding the pavement until he disappeared within seconds around the side of the building. Owen burst from the store, racing after the fleeing man.

Charles gave the brief thought to joining the chase, but knew with his injured leg, he didn't have a chance. Humiliation swept over him, but he managed to push it aside. Just because he didn't run as well as he used to, didn't make him less of a man. Besides, he needed to check on Demi. Her well-being was more important than chasing the man down.

Taking note in the direction the intruder fled, Charles turned back to the store and pulled open the door.

Stepping inside, he called out, "Demi?"

"In here."

Charles made his way through the darkened store toward Demi's voice. It sounded like it came from the small café area.

The lights came on and he blinked at the sudden brightness. "Whoa."

As his eyes focused, he took in Demi's frightened features. But she'd managed to find the fuse box and get the lights back on in spite of her fear. He went to her side and took her hands, feeling them tremble. "Are you all right?"

She nodded, eyes wide. "Someone was in here."

"I know," Charles said. "I saw him run out the back door and down the alley. Owen went after him. What happened?"

Pulling her hands from his grasp, she crossed her arms in front of her and rubbed them like she was cold. "I came down to get a book and heard something. The lights were out and didn't work. Then I heard…something. And he was there. Being quiet and watching…." She shivered and swallowed hard. Charles felt his heart clench at her distress.

The back door slammed and they both jumped. Charles's hand went to his weapon, his pulse spiking.

Owen called out, "It's just me." When Owen joined them in the kitchen, he shook his head in disgust and said, "I lost him."

Charles asked, "Do you think this has anything to do with the message left in the church?"

"I don't know." Owen narrowed his eyes. "You and I haven't really talked much about that. You think it was meant for you?"

"And I think it was meant for me," Demi said before Charles had a chance to answer.

"Why would you think that?" Owen looked confused.

Demi bit her lip then motioned for them to follow her.

Charles frowned as she and Owen walked up the steps to her apartment. She opened the door.

"You didn't lock the door?" Charles asked.

She paused then looked over her shoulder. "I didn't think I needed to. I was just going down to get a book and then come right back up. I thought the back door was secured and…" Demi fiddled with her keys. "I should have locked it, huh?"

"Yeah." Charles nodded.

He drew his weapon, glad he'd decided to start carrying it again. At Owen's sharp look, he shrugged. He had an up-to-date concealed weapons permit. Might as well exercise caution.

Owen nodded and took the lead, Charles providing backup. Demi stepped aside, her fear in full expression on her beautiful pale face. Behind her glasses, her eyes looked huge.

A quick sweep of the small apartment revealed nothing. "Clear," he said.

"Clear," Owen echoed.

Demi's quiet voice cut into the relieved silence. "Do you mind if I show you what I found yesterday morning? I think it'll explain why I think that message at church was for me."

"Sure."

Both men holstered their weapons.

Demi walked into the kitchen, opened the cabinet and pulled a coffee canister from the cupboard. She took off the lid and held the can out for the men to peer into.

Charles read the message on the piece of paper and felt his heart pick up speed.

Owen lifted a brow and looked at the two of them. "You found this yesterday?"

"And you didn't say anything?" Charles demanded. The words exploded from him. He couldn't help it.

She flinched and stepped back and Charles felt immediate remorse. "I'm sorry, I didn't mean to yell. But you really should have told someone about this."

"I meant to, I just…didn't. I wanted to think about it and try to figure out why someone would put that there. But all I get is a massive headache when I try to reason through it." She swallowed and met his eyes. "And I was afraid you'd blame yourself." Her

eyes slid away. "And that you'd ask me to leave."
She shrugged. "I didn't want to leave."

"Ah, Demi…." Charles sighed, guilt exploding
through him. She'd been right about that anyway.
He did blame himself for putting her in this situation.

Owen shook his head. "Have you touched this?"

"No." She grimaced. "I just slapped the top back
on and determined to put it out of my mind for the
day."

Owen asked, "Do you have a paper bag I can put
this in?"

"I have a plastic grocery bag."

"It'll have to do."

Demi got the bag and held it open.

Charles reached for the salad tongs sitting in the
container on the counter, pulled out the note and
dropped it in. He looked at Owen. "You really think
you can get anything off of that?"

"Thanks to new technology, fingerprints are
easier than ever to lift. Matching them up is sometimes the problem. But we'll give it a shot." He
looked at the can. "Let's throw that in, too. Has
anyone besides you touched it?"

"Not here. Fiona gave it to me. I think she got it
from the café, so…"

Owen nodded. "It's probably a long shot, but we
can try. Let's put it in a separate bag."

Demi got another bag and placed the can inside.

Owen said, "Charles has told me some details about your past when he had me run a background check on you before hiring you. Of course, there wasn't anything to learn because it was on the name you were given in the hospital. Can you fill me in a little better?"

She took a deep breath. "I'm not sure. Like I said, I don't remember what happened." She dropped her eyes then looked back up at him. "I can tell you what I was told."

"If you don't mind sharing that. Start from the beginning."

Demi nodded. "I was found on a street after dark in a back alley in Springfield, Massachusetts. I had several bad head wounds. I had no identification on me and no one had reported me missing." Reaching up, she pulled the glasses from her face and looked at them. "They found my glasses next to me. One of the officers came to see me in the hospital and said it looked like someone had deliberately crushed them. He wanted to know what I'd done to make someone so angry." Tears filled her eyes.

Charles wanted to punch his brother for asking her to relive that. But if it helped them find a clue to her past, he supposed it had to be done.

Blinking back tears, she said, "The police put my picture on the news and asked for information about my attack. But again, no one came forward to identify me—or offer any information."

Charles felt his heart twist once again. "That must have been awful. I'm so sorry."

She nodded. "Beyond awful. I healed pretty fast physically even though I was in the hospital for a couple of weeks. When it came time for me to leave, I just wanted to get away. So I went to the library, did a little research and found Fitzgerald Bay. I got on the bus—" she spread her hands "—and here I am."

Owen clicked his pen and put his little notebook in his back pocket. "All right. I'll see if I can find anything in any of what you've told me to help track down your identity." He left with promises to stay in touch with any news.

Charles turned to Demi. "So someone was in your apartment that day."

"It looks like it."

In an unexpected move, he pulled her to him for a hug. He was almost surprised that she didn't resist. Instead, she settled her head on his shoulder with a small sigh.

His hand raised up to give her a comforting pat on the back but then he found himself cupping her chin tilting her head to look up at him.

Questions danced in her eyes along with a look he interpreted as wariness. Immediately, he let her go and cleared his throat. She was right to be wary, to be cautious. She didn't know who she was or whom she might belong to. The lack of a ring on her left hand didn't mean there wasn't a wedding license in some drawer somewhere.

He cleared his throat. "If you're all right, I think I'll take off."

He saw her swallow. But she nodded. "I'll be fine."

With one last lingering look, Charles let himself out of the apartment and waited until he heard the lock click into place. Then he leaned against the wall and pulled in a steadying breath.

He decided coming face-to-face with Olivia's murderer wouldn't shake him up any more than his growing feelings for the woman behind that door.

NINE

"I'm not seeing him, he's a murderer."

Charles Fitzgerald overheard the elderly woman's comment and closed his fist around the pen he'd just used to sign his name. Not exactly how he wanted to start his Monday morning.

Another unhappy patient.

There'd been a lot of them. As a result, the practice had suffered. He'd called in a favor from a med school buddy to come work with him and help keep the practice from going under. It worked, but left Charles with more free time than he liked. And now he had another patient refusing to see him because of this cloud still hanging over his head.

He'd hoped this week would be different. Apparently last week was an aberration. Things had started out wonderful this morning. The minute Demi had stepped into his house, the children laughed and chattered a mile a minute. She'd grinned and waved him on his way.

Arriving at the office with a smile on his face

hadn't happened in a long time. Since Olivia's death and the string of accusations that had followed.

The smile had faded as the first person in the waiting room realized Charles would be his physician and mumbled he was feeling better. The man couldn't move fast enough to get out the door.

Things had been heading south ever since.

And now this.

If something didn't break soon in the investigation into Olivia Henry's death, his mind might be the first thing to snap.

Being under suspicion of murder for the past four months had gotten old fast. But it sure made clear who his friends were. And weren't.

"Ma'am." His secretary, Cecily Cross, couldn't have been more professional although Charles knew her well enough to hear the underlying thread of steel in her tone. "There's no evidence that Dr. Fitzgerald had anything to do with it or he'd be sitting in jail. He's a highly skilled doctor who has an open appointment. If you don't want to see him, we'll have to reschedule you with another appointment."

"I was told Dr. Hansen would see me."

"And I told you he called in and said he couldn't be here. He had a family emergency." Cecily's exasperation with the woman finally peeked through. Charles caught her eye and waved his understanding. He saw Cecily draw in a deep breath and get her thinly veiled indignation under control. "Fine." Cecily consulted the computer in front of her. "How about Wednesday morning at nine o'clock?"

The woman gave a disgusted moan, but nodded, "Very well. I suppose it's not an emergency. Please tell Dr. Hansen I'll be here at nine sharp and I expect him here, too." With a nod and a sniff of disdain, Mrs. Bertha Gold turned and toddled out the door.

Cecily eyed him from behind the desk. "You're too nice to people like that."

Charles sighed. "I can't do anything about Mrs. Gold and her attitude. I suppose until it's proven without a shadow of a doubt that I didn't have anything to do with Olivia's death, I'm just going to have to deal with that kind of stuff." He shrugged. "I'm getting used to it."

But he wasn't. The brave face he showed to the world hid his hurt and shame that people he thought were friends would believe him capable of such a thing. And truth be known, the longer this dragged out, the harder it was to keep the faith that the real murderer would be found.

Faith. Sometimes God seemed so far away. But, if Charles were honest, it was because he'd pushed Him away. The initial devastation he'd felt with Kathleen's abandonment had morphed into an anger that God hadn't stopped her from leaving. Now that Charles had healed from the hurt of his divorce, he wondered why it was harder to forgive God than it had been to forgive Kathleen.

Because Kathleen was human. She was supposed to make mistakes.

But God was perfect. And He could have stopped it all from happening. Just like He could reveal Olivia's murderer and end all the anguish Charles was now going through.

"Charles? You okay?"

He jerked, realizing he'd been standing there, staring at the door Mrs. Gold had exited. "Yes, sorry. I'll be in my office working on the files. Let me know if there's anything you need."

Cecily shook her head and muttered under her breath something about being innocent until proven guilty. Charles appreciated the woman's loyalty, but couldn't help wondering if he wouldn't feel the same way if the shoe were on the other foot. Would he be so judgmental if it had happened to one of his friends? He hoped not.

Back in his office, Charles picked up the picture of his children. Aaron and Brianne were his world. Thank goodness they weren't old enough to understand what was going on with their father.

His cell phone buzzed, interrupting his depressing train of thought.

"Hello?"

"Hey, it's Owen."

"What's up?"

"Just wanted to see if we were still on for a fishing trip sometime soon. I think we all need a break."

Charles shuddered. He didn't want Owen taking a break. He wanted to know who had killed Olivia. Forcing some levity into his voice, he said, "Sure." But he couldn't help asking, "Anything on the case?" No need to specify which one.

When Olivia had been found dead and he'd first been questioned, he'd been sure that the case would be wrapped up quickly and life would return to normal.

But it seemed like Olivia's murderer had been careful and clever.

Owen's heavy sigh didn't lift his spirits. "No. But we're working on it basically day and night. You know that. I called the lab ten minutes ago, pushing them to get us those DNA results. I feel certain that's the key in clearing you. Unfortunately, they're backlogged and we're waiting our turn in line. But they promised us no more than a week. A week, Charles, and you'll be cleared, all right? I've said it before and I'll say it again, we're going to get the creep who did this."

"I know. It's just…"

"No need to explain. I understand." Owen changed the subject. "How are the twins? I guess they didn't miss you last night."

"No, they were still sleeping when I got home."

"Well, Paige wants to see them again soon. She had a blast with them yesterday."

Paige. Owen's nine-year-old daughter. The daughter he'd just discovered and was building a relationship with.

"They're great. They love Demi and are perfectly happy with their little world. I'll bring them by the bookstore soon and Paige can read them a story or something while I have a cup of coffee or catch up on some sleep in one of those big comfy reading chairs."

Owen laughed then sobered. "Sorry it's taking us so long to figure this out, bro."

"Yeah, me, too."

"But hang in there, we'll get it done."

"I know." He paused. "Any calls after Demi's picture went up?"

"Yeah. We're sorting through them. When you do something like that, all the weirdos come out of hiding." Charles winced.

"So," Owen said. "Douglas and Merry are getting married in two weeks. Let's try to make the fishing trip before then."

"I'll look at my schedule and let you know."

Owen hung up and Charles dropped his head in his hands. Closing his eyes, he drew in a deep breath and prayed out loud, "Lord, I know I haven't been very talkative lately, but I'm thinking that's a mistake. Please help me out here, if You would. I really need a break somewhere."

Demi really needed a break. Not from the children or her job, but from her thoughts. "Hey, guys," she said to the kids who were digging in the sand. "What do you say we get cleaned up and go into town to get some ice cream?"

"Ice cream!" Brianne was the first to respond. Of course. Demi laughed.

"Dino, too." Aaron held out the toy to her.

"Does Dino want ice cream?" she asked.

He grinned and nodded.

"All right, let's go. Everyone on the bicycle." Charles had provided her with a double-stroller-like contraption that could be pulled behind her bicycle. She'd used it often last week when they got antsy or sleepy. Helmets on and strapped in, the twins sang a song about ice cream while Demi pulled out the cell phone Charles had given her and pressed the number one. Charles had programmed his cell number for her. He answered on the third ring. "Hello?"

"Hi, how's it going?"

"It's going."

Demi frowned at his tone. He sounded…frustrated. "I don't know how busy you are, but I thought I'd let you know that I'm taking the children up to the Sugar Plum Café for a scoop of ice cream."

"Are they wiggle worms today?" The frustration had disappeared to be replaced with a warmth that entered his voice every time he referred to his children.

Demi relaxed a bit as she swung a leg over the seat and got herself situated. "They are, but they're excited about the ice cream."

He paused. "I'll meet you there. I could use a break."

"Really?"

"Actually no. I've had a pretty long break already, but I need to get out of here. See you in a few minutes and be careful."

"Will do."

She hung up and looked back at her little charges all buckled in to ensure their safety. Blankets tucked in around them would keep them warm from the cool morning wind. "Ready?"

"Ready!" they yelled in unison.

Demi pressed the pedal and they were off.

Ten minutes later, she directed the bicycle into the parking lot of the Sugar Plum Café.

It was eleven o'clock and the lunch crowd had already started filing in. But she knew there'd be a spot in there somewhere for her, Charles and the children.

Unbuckling them, she took a little hand in each of hers and together they walked toward the door.

"Hey, wait up!"

Demi looked over her shoulder and felt her heart give a little skip when she saw Charles, still in his white lab coat, heading their way.

"Daddy!" Brianne pulled from Demi and launched herself at her father. He caught her in a hug and kissed the top of her dark head.

Aaron seemed content to watch their exuberance. Demi had a moment where her world spun around her and she pictured herself doing the very thing Brianne had done. Only she was throwing herself into Charles's arms to receive his kiss on her lips. A *welcome home, I'm glad to see you* kind of thing.

"Demi? You okay?"

His question burst her daydream and she could feel a flush creeping into her cheeks. Turning toward the store to hide the fire in her face, she said, "I'm great. Let's get that ice cream."

Once they got the children settled in high chairs with bibs and a large supply of napkins, they started in on the treat.

Brianne managed to get most of hers in her mouth. Aaron wasn't having much luck. Demi took his spoon to help him. She looked at Charles. "Has Owen run my picture on the news yet?"

He nodded. "Yes, Owen said they were filtering the calls. When they get something worth following up on, we'll be the first to know."

Demi bit her lip and slid another small spoonful

of vanilla ice cream into Aaron's waiting mouth. "Good. I think."

"It will be."

"Did he mention that I have amnesia?"

"No, he didn't want to invite any troublemakers or people who might want to take advantage of you. Instead, they ran the picture with the story that you were looking for your family and if anyone recognized you and knew who your family was, they were to call the eight hundred number at the bottom of the screen. As it is, we may have to weed through some crazies."

Demi grimaced. She hadn't thought about that. When the police had run her picture while she'd been in the hospital, she hadn't even considered that scenario. The police must have made the judgment calls in that case, too.

"Well, if this isn't a nice cozy scene."

Demi froze as she recognized the voice of Burke Hennessy. She glanced up to see him bearing down on their table.

Charles's posture went rigid. Demi ignored Hennessy and concentrated on feeding Aaron, hoping the children didn't pick up on the sudden tension.

"What do you want now, Burke?" Charles asked.

"Don't you have patients to take care of, Dr. Fitzgerald?" He didn't give Charles a chance to answer before he said, "Oh, that's right. You're a murder suspect. I imagine not too many people in town are in need of your services these days."

Charles's face went red and his hand clenched.

Demi looked at the man who seemed to have nothing better to do than cause trouble. "Could you please just leave us alone?"

Burke snorted. "Hiding behind a skirt? Who taught you that, your dad?"

Charles stood. "Burke, I'd like nothing more than to smash your face, but I'm praying real hard that I have more class than that. If you want to take this outside, I'll go, but you might want to think twice about how that will look to your constituents."

Demi blinked at the lightning-fast speed at which Burke backpedaled, his hands held in a conciliatory gesture. "Hey, no need for that." Then he dropped his hands and his eyes hardened. "But you can tell your father that I'm calling him out in a debate. I've had enough of this Fitzgerald monopoly in the police department and the town. Tell your father I'll be in touch."

Burke spun on his heel and left, seemingly unaware of the eyes that followed him. Charles cleared his throat and seated himself in front of Brianne. His daughter frowned. "Bad man, Daddy. Don't like him."

Demi choked back a surge of laughter, not thinking it was an appropriate response. Then she caught the glint in Charles's eyes as he nodded to Brianne. "Very observant young lady."

Brianne grinned as though she understood and Demi's heart softened at the exchange. She glanced at the door where Hennessy had just left. "I admire your restraint," she said softly.

Charles nodded his head. "Me, too." Pulling in a deep breath, he let it out slowly. Demi watched him for a moment longer, wishing she had the right words to say. Having none, she stayed silent.

He looked up and said, "How do you feel about fishing?"

She shrugged. "I don't know. Why?"

"Because I think that might be just the thing to take our minds off everything that's going on around here."

"And your mind off Burke Hennessy?"

"Exactly."

"Sounds good to me." She smiled then shivered as her eyes caught Burke's staring back at them from outside the restaurant window.

His malevolent glare said he wasn't finished with them.

TEN

Surprisingly, the rest of the week and most of the next passed without incident. Thursday rolled around with no more break-ins, no more weird messages. And nothing on Demi's true identity.

It made Charles nervous, but relieved, too. Maybe whoever had been causing problems decided to move on to something else.

The twist in his gut told him he could hope for that, but not to stop watching his—or Demi's—back just yet.

And the DNA results *still* hadn't come in.

Owen said that he and their father were nagging the lab, promising to leave them alone as soon as they passed on the results. So far there'd been no word. Charles refused to get his hopes up that they would come through any time soon.

He gathered his fishing equipment from his garage and turned to see Owen's orange Ford Raptor pickup pull into the drive. Victoria and their nine-year-old daughter, Paige, were with him.

Demi rode up on her bike just then and Charles found his attention centered on her. With wind-blown hair and pink cheeks, she looked about eighteen years old. He gulped then caught the knowing glint in Owen's eyes.

Feeling the heat creep up his neck he focused on loading the equipment into the back of his truck. "Morning," he called over his shoulder.

Demi parked the bike and greeted his brother and Victoria. Paige hopped out and slammed the door. "Can I help get the twins ready?"

"They're already in their car seats." Charles offered his niece a grin. "It was the only way *I* could get stuff ready."

Demi smiled. "I could have come a little early and helped."

"I appreciate that, but they're in a good mood this morning so I handled it." He turned to Paige. "But you can entertain them."

The girl gave an eager nod and climbed in the car where she was greeted with two-year-old squeals of glee.

Charles felt the hair on the back of his neck spike and he glanced around. All morning, he'd felt the presence of someone lurking, spying, and the feeling was getting old. He didn't spook easily, but the thought of someone watching him and the children made him jumpy.

He stared toward the cliffs where Olivia had fallen to her death and shuddered.

"Something wrong?"

Owen's perceptive question made Charles blink and he forced a smile. "Nope. Not a thing. Let's go have some fun."

"I called Dad and told him we needed an extra rod for Demi. He said he had one hanging in the storage building behind his house and to stop by and pick it up."

"Sounds like a plan to me."

Demi stashed the bike in the garage and climbed in the vehicle with him. Paige decided to ride buckled in between the twins.

Charles cranked the truck and headed to his dad's house. The sun continued to creep higher in the morning sky and the day promised to be a warm one. They'd shed their jackets in a couple hours, relax and maybe catch a fish or two.

A perfect day made even better because of the woman sitting beside him. "I'm glad you wanted to come with us. It took a little longer to get this trip lined up, working around Owen's schedule and Victoria's need to find someone to cover the shop, but I'm glad you decided you'd come."

Demi smiled. "Sure. I don't know if I've ever gone fishing before, but the adventure sounded too good to pass up."

He laughed. "Yes, I'm sure *adventure* is the right word for it."

A few minutes later, they pulled into his father's drive. "Sit tight. I'll just go in and get the rod."

Demi nodded and Charles climbed from the vehicle.

Owen met him. "I want to get some tackle, too."

Together the brothers entered the building and Charles went for the rods hanging on the wall while Owen opened the steel cabinet attached to the back wall.

Charles found a rod he thought Demi could use and turned to find Owen holding something and frowning at it. "What's wrong?"

"These."

Curious, Charles walked over for a look.

Several pictures of a couple, one holding a baby, stared back at him. "Where'd you find those?"

"In Dad's tackle box on the bottom under a bunch of fishing stuff."

Owen flipped through them, his face paling with each one.

Charles took them and did the same. He swallowed hard. Several showed a man and a pregnant woman in various poses. In one, the man had his hand possessively on the belly of the young woman, a grin on his face. He flipped the picture over and read, "My little one. Boy or girl?"

And then there was the picture of the man and woman holding a baby. No names or a date on the back.

"Hey, what's taking so long?" Victoria asked from the door. "The natives are getting restless."

Owen turned to her and held out the picture. "Look at this."

With a question in her eyes, Victoria took the photo and looked at it. Then her brows pulled together at the bridge of her nose. "Why does this picture look so familiar—like I've seen it before?"

"Where would you have seen this?" Charles asked.

"I'm not sure, but..."

Charles's heart thudded, dread coursing through him. His eyes met Owen's. "Is it possible?"

Owen swallowed hard. "You thinking what I'm thinking?"

"An affair?" Just saying the words left a foul taste in his mouth.

"A what?" Victoria sputtered.

"This is Dad in the picture, Victoria," Owen said.

She squinted. "Really?" A pause. "I didn't see it at first, but yes, the resemblance is there."

"And the woman he has his arm around is not Mom," Charles said.

"Who's the baby?" Owen asked quietly. "You don't think..."

Victoria gaped as she took in what Owen was saying. "That doesn't mean that your father..."

"…had an affair or that we have a half sibling," Charles finished the sentence for her.

Owen looked at Charles. "That's true. We don't know who this woman in the photograph is." He paced from one end of the toolshed to the other. Then he spun and jabbed a finger at Charles. "Just like I don't believe you killed Olivia, I don't believe Dad cheated on Mom."

Charles sucked in another breath. "You think I want to believe it? There's no evidence pointing to me being a killer." He shook the picture. "This just raises some questions, that's all."

Owen ran a hand down his face. "I don't know. I just…don't know."

"Looks like we have something to talk to Dad about. And soon."

"No," Victoria protested. "Not yet. Douglas and Merry are getting married this weekend. Don't ruin the wedding for them."

Charles paused, his heart thumping with adrenaline. This possibility of an affair, a half sibling, if it was true, sucked the air from his lungs. "I don't know. This is pretty serious stuff."

"I agree," Owen said. "I want some answers." He pulled out his cell phone and dialed his father's number. Charles waited impatiently.

Finally, Owen said, "Hey, Dad, give me a call when you get a chance, will you? We need to talk."

He hung up and rubbed a hand down his suddenly haggard face. Charles suddenly wasn't much in the mood for fishing.

Demi didn't mind waiting in the truck, but she wondered what was taking them so long in the shed. Tears spilled down Brianne's cheeks as she kicked her feet. "I want out!"

"Don't you want to go fishing?" Paige asked.

"No!"

Demi stepped from the truck, ready to release the child from her car-seat prison when she saw Charles, Owen and Victoria exit the shed. Charles carried the fishing pole while Owen tucked something into his shirt pocket.

Victoria looked shaken and pale.

What had happened?

Everyone climbed into their respective vehicles. Charles placed the fishing rod in the back and the troubled, tight look on his face worried her. After pacifying Brianne with a peanut-butter cracker, Demi looked at Charles. "What's wrong?"

He glanced in the rearview mirror. "I just need to process something before we talk about it, all right?"

Demi bit her lip. "Sure." He didn't want to talk in front of Paige.

But for her, some of the excitement of the day had

dimmed in light of whatever had happened in the storage building.

They rode in silence, broken only by the chattering of the children and Paige's exuberance at fishing in the river. "It's going to be so much fun!"

"I think it's funny that we're going out into the woods to find a river to fish when there's a whole ocean with a pier practically in your backyard," Demi teased.

Some of Charles's tension seemed to ease from his shoulders as he shot her a forced smile. "It's a place with a lot of memories. I grew up going fishing in this little spot. You'll love it."

"I'm sure I will."

Ten minutes later, Charles pulled into a clearing. Demi could see the path that led down to the river. Stepping down from the truck, she helped get the children out of the car seats and grabbed a folding chair. The men loaded themselves with all the fishing paraphernalia and Victoria lugged a rolling cooler behind her.

Paige helped with Aaron while Demi took charge of Brianne. Bringing up the rear, she let Brianne study her surroundings. The little girl clapped her hands and walked to the edge of the path.

"Ladybug," the little girl said.

"Where?"

"There." She pointed to a leaf where the insect sunned itself.

"She's pretty, isn't she?"

"Pretty," Brianne agreed, her black pigtails swinging back and forth with the movement of her head.

A twig snapped behind her and Demi turned.

Empty space stared back at her.

Demi turned to Brianne who still watched the little insect with fascination.

A rustle in the bush next to her made her jump and spin.

She could see nothing to cause her alarm, but the hair on her arms lifted and her heart thumped a little faster.

A shivering sensation slid along her spine and suddenly she realized how far ahead the others had gotten. She picked up Brianne in her arms. "Come on, sweetie, let's go catch a fish."

"Want the bug."

"Maybe we can find another one."

"Want that one."

Demi carried the little girl who was willing to be distracted with the idea of catching a fish. As she walked the path through the overgrown trees, following where the others had walked only moments before, she cast a glance over her shoulder.

Still she could see nothing and no reason to be alarmed.

But another rustling to her left made her flinch.

She picked up her pace and within seconds saw Charles's broad back. Relief filled her as she set

Brianne down on the blanket someone had placed on the ground.

"Are you okay?" Charles asked.

Demi smiled. She didn't want to sound silly about thinking someone had been behind her, so she said, "I'm great. When do we get to fish?"

The corners of his eyes crinkled. "Soon."

For the next half hour, Demi was able to put the creepy feelings aside and concentrate on having a good time with the Fitzgerald family.

With her line dangling in the river, her eyes on Charles and Owen as each man held a child, helping cast and reel to the children's excitement, she felt peaceful, content for the first time in a long time.

Leaning toward Victoria, she asked, "I have a question."

"Sure."

"Brianne spotted a ladybug on the trail out here and was fascinated with it." Demi held up an empty plastic container. "I thought I'd go find her one she could keep for a few days."

Victoria smiled. "What a great idea."

"I'll be right back."

Demi walked into the trees, studying each leaf, still wondering how she'd found herself in the midst of such a wonderful family.

She walked a good ways then stopped, remembering the creepiness she'd felt earlier. The feeling of being followed and watched. She supposed she could attribute the noises to an animal in the woods, but…

Nerves rippling, she glanced around. No animals, no strangers, nothing. Just her and the privacy of the woods.

And a pretty little black-and-red ladybug sitting on the leaf near her nose. Smiling, she scooped the little bug in the container, picturing Brianne's excited glee.

She turned to return to the river, but stopped as she realized she wasn't quite sure where she was.

The uneasiness in the pit of her stomach returned. Had someone followed them? Followed her?

The longer she stood there, the more the ominous feeling grew. Spinning, she hurried in the direction of the river.

At least she thought it was the right direction.

As she walked, she realized she'd gotten turned around. Sighing in frustration, she turned again and walked in the opposite direction.

Only to come to a small clearing that she didn't recognize. "Well, that's not right," she whispered to herself.

Heart thudding, Demi stopped and stood still.

The woods were never truly silent, but she couldn't hear laughter from those she'd come with. Closing her eyes, she focused her attention on listening.

And heard the faint sound of the water to her right.

Relieved, she took a step in that direction.

A branch snapped. A bush rustled. She stopped and stood still once again.

The hair on the back of her neck rose, her stomach twisted.

And she felt someone watching her.

At the edge of the clearing, just as she took her first running step toward the sound of the water, she felt a vise clamp around her upper arm and a hand slap over her mouth.

Fear scattered her senses. A scream gathered in her throat. Instinct kicked in and she tried to jerk away. But he was strong. Blood hit her tongue as she twisted against him. His hand slipped and she pulled in a breath.

ELEVEN

Charles glanced at the shoreline one more time. His waders kept his pants dry but the mud sucked at the bottoms of his feet. He didn't care, he was having a great time, relaxing and enjoying the afternoon with his family—and Demi.

Marred only by the knowledge that his father might have had an affair. And a child.

Another glance in the direction Demi'd disappeared made him frown. He'd watched the exchange between Victoria and Demi and smiled when he saw her tromp into the woods. She was a trouper, willing to try anything, including roughing it a bit in his favorite fishing spot.

But she'd been gone awhile.

As the minutes stretched, so did his nerves.

He started envisioning all kinds of things that could happen. A snake bite, a black bear, a fox…a two-legged creature.

A restless worry hit him. He had to check on her.

Sloshing to the shore, he set his pole next to Victoria. She held a sleeping Brianne. The little girl had given up fishing and crawled in her future aunt's lap. "I guess that's why she was so cranky."

"Probably." Victoria shot a look toward the woods, her brow furrowed and eyes troubled. "I hope Demi's okay. She's been gone a long time."

"I noticed. I'm going to—"

The sharp scream cut him off.

"Demi!"

He and Owen exchanged a startled look. Charles said to Victoria, "Watch the kids."

Running toward the sound of the scream, heart thumping in his chest, the waders slowed him down a bit, but determination to get to her side spurred him on.

Crashing through the undergrowth, he slipped, tripped and caught himself. "Demi!" he shouted.

"Charles!" Her piercing cry called to him.

Her voice had came from the left. He turned, ran about a hundred yards and nearly tripped over Demi in a small clearing. She was sprawled on the ground, holding her arm. Blood from a cut on her lip glinted in the sun. A plastic container holding a ladybug lay to her right.

He rushed to her and dropped to a knee beside her. "Are you all right? What happened? Are you hurt?"

She touched her lip and winced. "A man grabbed

my arm from behind and slapped his hand across my mouth."

"Which way did he go?" Owen asked.

Charles looked up, startled. He hadn't realized his brother had followed him.

Demi raised a shaking hand and pointed to the woods behind her. "When I screamed, he still tried to drag me, but when he heard you shout, he shoved me away and ran. I turned to see if I could get a good look at his face, but he was too fast."

Owen exchanged a look with Charles. "I'll see what I can find."

He took off and Charles helped her to her feet. Leaning over her, he studied her lip and said, "Let me take a look at that."

"It's fine. When he covered my mouth, I bit my lip."

Still, he moved closer and narrowed his eyes as he ran a thumb over the uninjured area around her lip. "It's a slight abrasion. You'll have a sore there for a couple days, but it should heal pretty fast."

He saw her cheeks heat and realized how intimate his touch could be construed. Clearing his throat, he dropped his hand.

Owen's approach broke the tension. Then fear flashed back into her eyes and she gulped. Grateful for his brother's return, Charles asked, "Did you find anything?"

Using a broken stick, Owen held up a small scrap

of fabric about the size of a quarter. "I suppose this could be considered contaminating evidence but I didn't want to leave it out there. I found it hanging on a branch. It's possible it belongs to our guy. I've got a bag in my car. I'll send it to the lab when we get back."

Charles looked at Demi. She trembled and his gut clenched in anger at the person who'd done this to her. He couldn't help wonder if it was because of him.

Then again, the message in her coffee can said that might not be the case. "Maybe we should pack up and leave," Charles said as he rubbed a hand across his face, weariness seeping in. Would this madness never stop? What would it take to catch the person trying to terrorize him? And now Demi?

Guilt plagued him. Was this his fault? Had Demi's attacker somehow figured out that Charles was developing feelings for his new nanny and had decided to get at him through her?

He shuddered.

"No," Demi protested. "I don't want this to ruin the fun for this afternoon."

He noticed her trembling had stopped and her eyes glittered with something he hadn't seen before.

Determination.

Owen shook his head. "Let's get back to Victoria and the children. I don't want to leave them alone too much longer." He grabbed his cell phone.

"I'm going to get someone here to go through the woods. I want to make sure this person isn't living out here."

Demi rubbed her palms together. "I think he followed us."

Owen raised a brow. "Why do you think that?"

She shrugged. "I just do." She kept her gaze on Charles. "I think someone's targeted us for whatever reason and is doing his best to scare us or torment us. Or…whatever."

So, she was thinking along the same lines as he was. But was trying to be tactful about setting blame anywhere. He clenched his jaw. They both knew where the blame lay.

Owen eyed her. "And you still don't have any memory of anything?"

"No. I'm sorry."

He nodded. "You guys go on back. I'll wait here for the team that's coming. I want to show them where to look."

Charles took Demi's hand. "Come on, I'll take you to the river." He looked at Owen. "I don't like this one bit. You need to come up with a plan to catch this person."

Owen pursed his lips. "Working on it."

Charles grunted. Owen may be working on it, but Charles decided if he had to, he'd take matters into his own hands.

Because no one was going to hurt Demi just because she'd had the misfortune to be in his life.

Demi was relieved to see the children playing a game of tag, unaffected by her recent misadventure. Victoria, however, looked strained. When she saw Demi and Charles heading her way, she jumped up. "What happened?"

"Demi was attacked in the woods."

Victoria gasped and grasped Demi's arm. "Are you all right? Here. Sit down and tell me what happened."

While Demi filled her in, Charles joined in the game. Then he gathered the twins and Paige, challenging them to a contest of who could catch the biggest fish.

Demi's heart melted as she watched him with the children. Her fear dissipated slightly. She could feel Victoria's gaze on her.

Keeping her voice low so Charles couldn't hear, she said, "Someone's really out to hurt Charles, I think."

"Why do you say that?"

Demi gave a slight shrug, wincing at the pull of a strained shoulder muscle. "I think the person who killed Olivia may get away with murder because no one is focusing on finding the real killer. Whoever is causing Charles and me all this trouble may think he's doing the authorities a favor."

"You mean, he thinks that if he pushes Charles hard enough, Charles will admit to the murder?"

A sigh slipped out before she could repress it. "Who knows? I think it's possible."

Victoria nodded, her eyes on Owen and Paige, the tender expression catching at Demi's heart. Then Victoria said, "It makes sense." She turned and caught Demi's gaze. "It's obvious Charles cares about you. Even in the short amount of time I've spent around you two, it's clear that he has feelings for you."

Demi gulped at the woman's observation. What could she say? It was true. And she definitely had developed feelings for Charles. Victoria gave her a small smile. "I think it's great."

"You do?"

"Sure. Charles needs someone like you in his life. He has for a long time." She bit her lip then said, "Just try not to hurt him."

Demi let her gaze rest on Charles. She smiled as he did his best to keep a wiggling Brianne from slipping from his grasp and into the water.

"Hurting Charles is the last thing I want to do. I promise."

"I catch it, Daddy." Brianne set her little mouth in firm determination and did her best to cast her rod. Aaron copied his sister and Paige giggled.

As the three waded back into the water, Demi caught Charles's gaze, pulled in a deep breath and prayed nothing else would happen to destroy their peace of mind.

Owen stepped from the edge of the woods and Demi tensed. She stood and walked over to him. "Did you find anything?"

"Nothing. I'm sorry. Just that scrap of material that I sent with one of the guys to the lab."

She nodded and bit her lip.

A cry from behind made her whirl, wondering what was wrong now.

But it was a happy cry. Brianne giggled and clapped as her daddy helped her pull in a decent-size fish. Aaron cheered his sister's success and Paige gave a mock pout. "It's my turn to fish with Uncle Charles. He's the only one catching anything around here."

Owen shot her a look that promised he wouldn't forget about her. Then he raced toward his daughter and caught her around the waist. "I should toss you in the water for that comment, squirt."

Paige let out a squeal and Demi walked over to settle on the blanket next to Victoria who patted her back. "Don't worry, Demi, the Fitzgeralds will figure this out."

"I know." And she felt sure they would. In time.

But would it be before anyone else got hurt? Or worse?

Night fell and Charles paced the floor as he waited for his brother Ryan to come back on the line. Just as Charles had answered the phone, Ryan's other line had rung and he'd put Charles on hold.

So now he waited, impatience twisting inside him.

Demi and Mrs. Mulrooney, his father's housekeeper, had volunteered to tuck the twins in and Charles had let them with a grateful heart. Mrs. Mulrooney had been at the house, putting a casserole in his refrigerator when they'd walked in the door several hours ago.

Charles had to admit he didn't know what he'd do without the woman who was supposed to be his *father's* housekeeper, but she seemed to enjoy doting on him, too. The twins adored her and if she hadn't said keeping up with them was too taxing at her age, he would have been content to let her be the children's nanny.

But she wouldn't have been up for hours of fishing like Demi had been.

They'd finished the day, doing their best to put on happy faces for the children while catching a few fish, but there was no denying it had been tainted for the adults thanks to the attack on Demi.

Ryan finally came back on the line and said, "Owen had to take care of something and asked me to give you a call. They didn't find much in the woods where Demi was attacked other than some broken branches where it looks like someone was in a hurry to leave. No footprints on that ground, of course, but we sent the fabric Owen found to the lab. Hopefully we'll hear something before too long."

Charles blew out a sigh. Nothing he hadn't expected. "Thanks for letting me know."

"Sure. We're not giving up and we're running Demi's picture on the news again asking for someone to come forward if they know her or any family members."

"Good. I can't believe there's absolutely no one who knows her."

"Someone will turn up."

"Someone legit, let's hope."

"Yeah."

Ryan hung up and Charles realized he and Owen still needed to talk to their father. And he still needed to get Demi home.

Even though it wasn't dark yet, there was no way he was letting her walk or ride her bike home by herself.

She and Mrs. Mulrooney came into the den. Demi flopped onto the couch and Mrs. Mulrooney picked up her keys.

Charles stopped her. "I hate to ask, but would you mind staying with the children while I run Demi home?"

The woman smiled and placed her keys back on the small table in the foyer. "I'd be glad to. They're so tired I doubt they'll stir." She eyed the recliner. "Might catch me a little nap myself."

Charles smiled. "Thanks." To Demi, he said, "I'll put the bike in the back of the truck. Ready?"

"I'm ready." She rose and gathered her bag.

Charles took her home. He noticed she didn't have a lot to say on the ride to The Reading Nook or even when he followed her up the stairs. But he did notice her increased nervousness the closer they got to her home.

"I'm going to check out your apartment, just to be on the safe side. Is that all right?"

They walked together as Charles inspected the shadows, the little hallway and the area around her door. All looked fine. He breathed a little easier.

She opened the door and stepped inside to flip on the light switch. As light bathed the room, he watched her shiver as she looked around. "It's kind of creepy staying here now." Chloe wrapped herself around Demi's ankles and Charles noticed the way she took comfort in the cat's affection.

He finished the short inspection then said, "Everything looks good, but I think I'm going to call Ryan and see if he'll okay a cruiser to watch the store. After everything that's happened, I don't think it'll be a problem."

Demi lifted a brow. "Have my own bodyguard?"

He nodded. "Something like that. Tonight Ryan said he'd have someone watching my house. I think it would be a good idea if he did the same here."

Her eyes went to the cabinet, now minus the coffee

can with the message. "It seems like someone has pretty easy access into my apartment, doesn't it?"

"Unfortunately. I think it's time to change the locks."

She nodded, her eyes troubled, scared.

Charles could almost see her brain processing the memory of the attack in the store and the one in the woods. He pulled out his cell phone and dialed Ryan's number.

His brother answered on the second ring. After making the arrangements, Charles hung up and said, "Someone's on the way. Ryan agreed it might be the smart thing to do."

She pulled in a deep breath, rubbed a cheek against Chloe's head then nodded. "As long as you think Fiona won't be upset with me. I don't want to chase away any customers."

"She'll understand. She'd much rather you be safe than sell a few books if that's what it comes down to. Besides, security is always a good thing."

Demi hesitated. "Well, it would be nice having him out there at night, but I don't think it's necessary during the day."

Charles touched her cheek, his concern for her safety embedded deep in his heart. "Demi, I know we've only known each other a short time, but I…" He stopped. What could he say? He was a murder suspect.

Her wide eyes told him to back off. She wasn't

ready for anything more than friendship and a professional working relationship. At least not yet.

Then her expression softened and she took his hand. "Charles, I think you're a wonderful man and a great father. But until I know who I am—" she shrugged "—I feel like I'm living in limbo. I mean I don't think I'm married." She shook her head and looked at her ringless hand. "I really don't. Somehow, I think I would know that. But I don't know if there's someone else or…" She trailed off with a sigh. "I just don't know."

He frowned. But he understood. "I know. And until this murder case is wrapped up, I'm right there with you, although in a different kind of way."

She walked to the window and looked out. "But the fact is, if I don't get my memory back soon, I'm going to have to make the decision to live with it and move on with my life. I can't live like this forever," she finished on a whisper.

"I agree." He followed her and placed a hand on her shoulder, hoping to offer comfort. He swallowed hard and turned her to face him. "Once this murder case is wrapped up, if you haven't gotten your memory back, or even if you have and there's no one…" He stopped and closed his eyes as he searched for the right words. "Just…after…you know? Could we…"

"Yes. After," she said, then bit her lip.

Elation filled him. She wasn't shutting the door on a possible relationship with him. "Good. After."

He left it at that.

"And on that note, I'll say good-night."

"Good night, Charles. I loved spending the day with you and the children in spite of…well, everything else."

Charles ran a finger down her soft cheek then turned to leave. He paused and swung back to say, "I know this is short notice, but would you go to Douglas and Merry's wedding with me on Saturday?"

She gave a gentle smile. "It's not after yet."

Charles stepped forward and took her warm fingers in his hand. "I know. But go to the wedding with me, then we'll worry about after…after that."

When she hesitated, he groaned. "Am I pushing you too much?"

"No. Not at all. I'd love to go to the wedding with you." A pause and a sigh. "And then, yes, we'll worry about after…after."

Charles pulled her to him in a hug, breathing in her scent, enjoying the feel of her in his arms, next to his heart.

Then he set her back from him, looked into her eyes and said, "After."

TWELVE

Early Friday morning, Demi stood at the window, sipping her coffee and pondering the fact that she had a police car sitting outside her home. Watching her.

Because she might be in danger.

Danger. She shivered.

This morning, that word brought back a sense of dread and fear she couldn't shake for more than a couple hours.

Although, she had to admit, she'd surprised herself and slept well last night after Charles had left. She'd expected to toss and turn. Instead, she'd felt safe, protected, because of Charles and his brother Ryan's willingness to put an officer outside.

And the fact that she now had shiny new locks on her door thanks to a friend of Charles's who'd arrived bright and early this morning to change them.

But she couldn't help wonder if it was a false sense of security. She also wondered if whoever was after her was watching and just waiting for the moment to make his move. Because he knew as well as she did that the time would come when she wouldn't have someone with her or her guard would be lowered. The police officer would leave soon and she would be alone again.

And what about riding to work on the bike? Would she be safe?

Her cell phone rang and she snatched it up after seeing Charles's number on the screen. "Good morning."

"Good morning." Just hearing his voice sent a different kind of shiver through her. Which worried her. Being attracted to him wasn't a bad thing. At least she didn't think so. However, she couldn't get the worry out of her head that she might have someone else in her life. Someone she might not be able to remember, but someone who remembered *her*.

Having no memory of herself was one thing. What if she couldn't remember someone she'd made a promise to? A husband. A boyfriend.

Was she betraying another man by having feelings for Charles?

The thought made her gulp. Just like she'd told Charles last night, she felt sure she would know that instinctively even if she couldn't actually remember it. Wouldn't she?

"Dad and Burke are meeting in the park at ten o'clock sharp to have some sort of debate that

Burke's come up with," Charles said. "It was on the news late last night. Victoria brought Paige over this morning to play with the twins and said she'd just bring them to the park. Do you mind meeting me there? My secretary called and said I have two last-minute appointments but I should finish in time to meet you."

She heard the relief in his voice. "Really? That's wonderful."

"Yes, it is. So, see you at ten?"

"I may be a little late, but I'll be there."

Ten o'clock rolled around fast. Demi soon found herself in the park along with a horde of people. Word spread fast in this little town. Reporters milled, waiting for the two candidates. She wondered if Judge Ronald Monroe would show up, as well. She'd heard something about him wanting to throw his hat into the ring, but hadn't yet done so simply because Aiden and Burke had so many supporters.

Demi kept an eye on the parking lot across the street. She figured Charles would meet Victoria to get the twins and then stroll over to her.

She caught sight of Aiden Fitzgerald and the rest of Charles's brothers and sisters. All but Fiona appeared to be here in an official capacity.

Because of the strong animosity between the two candidates, security was out in force. Uniforms and plain clothes patrolled the area. Her eyes landed on

Judge Monroe. He stood near the platform, looking thoughtful and troubled.

Microphones were set up behind two podiums, ready for the candidates to take the stage.

Demi saw Burke arrive with his wife, Christina, who held their toddler daughter, Georgina. He looked proud, confident and almost strutted as he approached the microphone.

Aiden looked determined, calm. In control. She had a feeling control was very important to Aiden and he would do anything to keep it—in all areas of his life. She wasn't sure why that stood out to her, but it did.

Charles strolled the children up beside her. Victoria waved as she and Paige headed toward Owen who stood near the stage. Demi waved back, a twinge of envy unsettling her as she watched Owen wrap an arm around his fiancée's shoulder and tweak Paige's nose.

However, when the twins saw her, their eyes brightened and Demi felt the envy subside. She dropped to her knees to greet each child with hugs and raspberries to their sweet cheeks. Their giggles rang in her ears.

Then she looked up at Charles and said, "I hope this goes well for your father."

His jaw went tight as he looked at the man. "Yes, me, too." He didn't sound like it, though.

"Something wrong?" she asked.

"Yes. Very wrong."

Concerned, she stood and laid a hand on his arm. "What?"

He sighed. "It's something I need to discuss with my father—a conversation I don't want to have."

"I'm sorry." She wondered if whatever it was had to do with what happened in the shed the day they went fishing. Ever since then, Charles's tension level seemed to rise whenever he was in his father's presence. He'd talked about needing to process something that day, too.

A voice from one of the podiums spoke, "As you are aware, we have two candidates running for mayor. Burke Hennessy and Aiden Fitzgerald. Burke has called this impromptu debate and we appreciate you all coming out."

He went on to introduce each man and then said, "I have a list of questions, given to me by various town members."

"This ought to be good," Charles muttered loud enough for her to hear.

It was crowded and people milled around her. A slender man in a gray hoodie caught her attention. He looked like the man who'd tried to get into her building last week. And the one she had seen on the beach. Curious, she moved toward him wanting to get a better look.

A hand caught hers and she looked back to see

Charles watching her with a question in his eyes. She pointed. "I think I've seen him before."

"Who?"

"That man in the hoodie."

Charles followed her pointing finger. "I don't see anyone."

She looked and the man was gone. A shiver slid up her spine. Who was he? And why did she feel like he was watching her? That he was here specifically because of her? The strange sensation refused to leave her alone even when she tried to reassure herself that no one would try anything in this crowd.

Then her attention was back on the debate that had started without her even noticing.

Burke gestured with his left hand. "And how can we want a mayor who is so lax in his current position as the police chief? One who can't even solve the murder of the young woman, Olivia Henry?"

"Now, wait a minute," Aiden protested.

"No, you wait a minute," Burke blustered as he jabbed a finger at Aiden. "Your own son is a suspect in the murder. Clearly, because he's your son, an arrest has not been made." Burke looked out at the audience. "Is this who you want for mayor? A man who allows his judgment to be impaired because he doesn't want to arrest his own son?"

Several people in the audience murmured among themselves. Those around Demi and Charles stared at him. She felt his tension magnify tenfold. Wrapping her fingers around his, she squeezed tight, hoping he got her message of support.

Aiden countered with, "And do you want a mayor who will order the arrest of a man when there's no evidence to back it up?"

And so it went back and forth for the next thirty minutes. Demi was amazed at the difference between the two men. Burke was all bluster and puffed-up pride. Aiden kept his cool and answered with thought and wisdom. The red in his cheeks said he kept a tight rein on his temper, but even that was far more impressive than Burke's lack of restraint.

She knew who she'd vote for. If she could vote. She frowned. The lack of identity was troubling in more ways than one.

"Come on," Charles said suddenly. "I need to get out of here."

"What is it?" Demi looked up to see a muscle jumping in Charles's cheek.

"Burke Hennessy gets to me. I can't watch this anymore."

A loud crack interrupted the ongoing argument at the podium. Demi gasped as something stung the flesh of her upper arm. And then she was surrounded by screaming people.

Another pop and the ground puffed up right where Charles had been standing a split second earlier. She felt an arm wrap around her waist and yank her down.

And then she realized it.

Someone was shooting at them!

"The babies!" she cried.

"Head for the cars, duck behind one," Charles hollered in her ear.

"Everybody down! Down! Shooter!" an officer to her right yelled.

Terror thumped a steady beat in her heart, as she turned to see Charles hunched over the twins' double stroller and she knew he'd take a bullet in order to protect the children.

Gasping, hurrying, she made her way to the nearest car and hunched behind several other people. Charles shoved the stroller next to her and dropped to his knees beside her.

Trembling, she tried to reassure the crying children that everything would be all right. Terrified screams echoed in her head, rattling her. The screams sounded familiar, as did the fear now coursing a steady path through her veins.

Brianne held out her arms and lunged for Demi, but trapped in her stroller, she couldn't get free. "Out! Out! Now!"

"I'll take you in a minute, baby," Demi gasped as she peeked around the tire to see what was happening. Her heart thundered, her lungs felt starved for air.

Law enforcement officials swarmed the area. She

thought she saw Ryan and Owen heading to the spot the bullets came from.

One more shot and Demi lurched back with a cry as the bullet pinged off the front bumper.

Charles shifted behind her. "Stay with the children."

"Where are you going?"

"Away from here to protect everyone. He's shooting at *me*."

Charles rushed from behind the safety of the vehicle, his limp more pronounced under the stress of the situation. He prayed that if he got far enough away from them, Demi and the children would be safe. That if the shooter couldn't spot his target, he would have no reason to shoot again.

The guy had shot twice into the crowd. The only reason he'd missed was because Charles moved and messed up his shot. The third time had nicked the car Charles'd been hiding behind.

He moved away from the crowd, his body taut, nerves humming. Who was the man shooting at him? One of Burke's hires?

Someone wanting revenge for Olivia's death and thought Charles was responsible? He kept moving, away from the crowd, his mind back in Iraq, prepared for anything.

His breathing came in pants, but his cool control never slipped. He'd been a medic, but he'd also trained as a soldier. He slipped into that mode now as easily as pulling on a comfortable shirt.

Darting behind a large SUV, he paused, heart thrumming, but his breathing was even, his senses on hyperalert.

He looked back to see Demi watching him with wide, scared eyes, but she held her body over the children.

The sight of her caring for them, protecting them as though they belonged to her, did something to his heart that he'd never felt before. Something he'd have to examine a little more closely at a later time.

Charles let his eyes scan the park, the buildings surrounding it. Numerous hiding places. But the shots had come from behind him. Probably from a higher floor where the shooter would have a good view of the park.

Already officers swarmed the buildings. More sirens sounded. Chaos ruled, but Charles didn't let that distract him.

He moved to the left, exposing himself for a brief second then slipped back behind his cover. Nothing happened. No shots rained down on him.

He let out a deep breath and wondered what that meant. Had the shooter been caught—or had he escaped?

Officers appeared, shaking their heads. He saw Ryan put his gun back into his holster.

Well, that answered that question. The shooter

was gone. Escaped. Free to return and cause trouble at another time. Trouble that Charles may not be able to dodge next time.

Not allowing himself to dwell on that possibility, Charles raced back to Demi and the kids. He wrapped an arm around her shoulders and reassured himself that she and his children were still in one piece.

Then he noticed the blood on her arm.

THIRTEEN

The stinging, burning sensation in her upper right arm started the minute she realized everyone was safe.

Wincing, she looked down to find blood. Her stomach clenched. Had she been shot?

Charles gently set her back. "Let me see."

Brianne and Aaron hollered and fought against their restraints while Charles probed the wound.

She winced. "It must not be too bad. I didn't notice it until now."

"Adrenaline. It can mask pain. I saw guys with limbs blown off and they didn't even realize it." She jerked and he grimaced. "Sorry. I shouldn't have said that."

"No, it's all right. It's a part of you."

His eyes caught hers. "Yes, I suppose it is. Not the part that I particularly like, but one I can't change."

Demi lifted her uninjured arm and reached up to wipe a smudge of dirt from his chin. "I wouldn't change one thing about you."

His eyes darkened and an emotion she couldn't identify flashed in them. He started to say something but Brianne's whiny cry interrupted him.

He turned from her and did his best to reassure the children before once again focusing his attention back on her arm.

"Are you all right?"

"Is she hit?"

The voices came from her left.

Demi looked up to see Ryan and Owen hovering, their concerned gazes on her and Charles. Charles spoke without turning. "She'll be fine. I think the bullet just grazed her. Either that or it ricocheted off something."

Ryan freed a screaming Brianne from her stroller and held her on a hip.

She quieted and lay a head on his shoulder. "Thank you, Unca Ryan."

"You're welcome, darlin'." He kissed the top of her dark head and Demi's heart twinged again. How close and loving this family was. Then she saw Ryan blanch as he said, "I think I know what it bounced off of."

His white face and grim tone alarmed her. Demi followed his gaze. And saw the metal handle of the stroller inches from where Aaron's head rested against the cushioned seat. She gasped and felt Charles's fingers tighten momentarily on her arm.

She ignored the flash of pain as the horror of what almost happened hit her.

"Oh, Charles…" she breathed, tears clogging her throat.

"They're fine. They're okay." She didn't know if he was saying the words to reassure her or himself. Probably both.

"We've got officers searching everywhere," Owen said. "He won't get far."

"Did you see him?" Charles asked, his voice low.

A pause. Then Owen said, "No. Not even a glimpse."

The two brothers stared at each other for a brief moment before Charles rubbed a hand down his face.

Ryan said, "Just more proof that God shows up even when bad stuff is happening."

"Yeah." Charles's voice sounded tight, strangled almost and Demi knew he was picturing what could have happened.

"As far as we could tell, there are no casualties. No one hurt except Demi," Owen said.

"That's because he was aiming at me." Charles's quiet statement rocked his brothers, Demi could tell.

But as the thought sank in, Owen nodded and said, "I can see why you would think that."

"I don't think it, I know it." Charles sighed and said, "Demi, your arm needs a bandage and you probably need some antibiotics just as a precaution.

Let's get over to my office and get that taken care of. We can sneak through the back alley. If anyone else connects that shooter to me, it's going to be crazy and I don't think I'm up to facing the media or a crowd of hysterical people right now."

Demi reached out for Aaron's hand and he clasped her fingers and said, "Want out."

"I know, darling. Just a little longer."

Ryan settled a protesting Brianne back into her seat. "We'll take care of this mess here. You duck out while you can. Like you said, if the media gets ahold of you, they're going to start asking questions about Olivia. You don't need that aggravation."

"No, I don't."

"Then get Demi taken care of and I'll fill you in on everything later. Let me have an officer escort you. If this guy is truly after you, we don't need to be sending you off all by yourself."

Charles's jaw went tight and Demi knew he didn't want an escort. Then she saw his eyes dart to his children. Then her. He gave a slow nod. "I won't argue with you. Might not be a bad idea to have some backup. Thanks."

"Good." Ryan nodded and spoke into his radio. He looked up and said, "Someone will be here in a minute."

True to his word, a uniformed officer soon rounded the corner of the building and joined them.

Ryan filled him in on what was needed. The young man nodded.

Charles took control of the stroller. His eyes landed on the dent left by the bullet and Demi saw him shudder.

She cradled her arm as she followed him toward his office. As they skirted the crowd, Demi saw the faces of the people. Shock, anger, terror. Emotions ran the gauntlet and the media grabbed every available emotional moment.

The walk seemed to take forever and she kept expecting someone to jump out and start shooting at them again. It didn't happen and soon she saw Charles's office come into view.

Once inside, Charles asked his secretary, Cecily, to watch the children. She agreed. Her eyes on the officer accompanying them, she asked, "What happened at the debate? I heard sirens. Sounded like the entire police force was out there."

"They were," Charles said. "Someone started shooting into the crowd." Cecily gasped and Charles continued, "Demi was hurt. I'm just going to take a look at her arm."

Still stunned, the woman nodded and released the restless children from the stroller. They darted to the play area with glee. The waiting room was empty. Apparently, the debate had been the priority for the majority of the citizens of Fitzgerald Bay, sick or not.

Charles was silent, his eyes troubled as he went about patching up her arm. She left him to his thoughts, not sure what to say, still in shock at everything that had happened in the past hour and a half.

With gentle hands, Charles put the final piece of tape on her arm.

"Are you allergic to anything?"

She blinked and sighed. "I have no idea."

"Right. We'll use a broad spectrum antibiotic, so you don't have to worry." He shook his head as he wrote the script. "Sometimes I forget…"

Demi smiled. "It's okay. Sometimes even I manage to forget for a little while."

"The wedding's tomorrow." He looked at her arm. "If you don't feel like going…"

"No, I'll be fine. I want to go."

Frowning, he said, "I just wonder if I should go."

"Because it looks like someone is out to get you?"

"Exactly." He shook his head. "My children, my family, everyone at the debate was in danger this morning because of me."

"You can't know that for sure."

"I'm pretty sure. There were three shots this morning. The first one missed only because I moved at the last second. The last two missed because of dumb luck, God looking out for me, I'm not sure which."

She looked at her wounded arm then back at him. "I prefer to think God's looking out for us."

His face softened. "Yeah, I'm getting to that point, too." Then his jaw tightened. "Well, today answered one question."

"What's that?"

"I thought Burke Hennessy might have been behind everything going on, but looks like he can't be held responsible for this incident."

"Unless he hired someone," she muttered.

Admiration glinted in his eyes. "Yes, there is that." Then he sighed. "I'll talk to Ryan about whether or not I should go to the wedding and let you know."

"Okay. But it would be a shame for you to miss it."

"Yes, it would. Douglas and Merry have been waiting for that day for a long time now." He reached up to stroke her cheek and she sucked in a deep breath. He swallowed. "Today was too close for comfort."

"I know," she whispered.

"I know we said we'd talk…after…but—" his throat worked "—I don't want to lose you, Demi."

Her heart clenched. What could she say? "I know, Charles. I don't want to lose you, either. I just…"

"I know." He gave her a small smile. "I'll be patient."

Her anxiety eased slightly. "Thanks."

"Yeah." He helped her down from the table. "Come on."

They walked back out to the waiting area where Brianne and Aaron still played. Brianne poured imaginary tea and Aaron fired his Dino from the top of the small television set. Dino landed in Brianne's cup and she hollered her anger while Aaron looked confused about what had triggered her wrath.

Charles immediately swooped in and picked up the little girl. Startled, Brianne squealed, then giggled, her ire forgotten.

But Charles's shadowed eyes hurt her heart and she wished there was something she could do.

Brianne said, "I want ice cream."

Charles allowed a glimmer of a smile to lighten his face. "I'm sure you do. I think after today we all might need some ice cream."

Brianne gave an eager nod. "Very good idea, Daddy. Yummy."

Just as they were gathering the children, Ryan stepped into the office.

Charles looked up. "Did you get him?"

"No. He got away."

"Anyone else hurt?"

Ryan shook his head. "Come with me. We need to talk."

Charles and Demi finished loading the protesting children into the stroller. Charles pushed and Demi followed Ryan out the door. The officer stayed with them, bringing up the rear.

Back on the street, Ryan led the way to the Sugar Plum Café where Owen and Victoria ushered them into an empty back room used to host large parties.

Victoria took charge of the children. "We're going to see Fiona at The Reading Nook."

Charles shot a look of gratitude toward his soon-to-be sister-in-law.

Owen looked at Charles. Under his breath and out of earshot of anyone else, he whispered, "I know this isn't the best timing, but we really need to talk to Dad about that picture."

"You're right, the timing stinks, but—"

Aiden opened the door and stepped inside. Charles clamped his lips together as his father said, "Have a seat. I've decided we needed a little impromptu meeting about what's going on with Charles." He settled into the nearest chair and looked at his son. "Someone appears to be of the mind to want you out of the picture."

Charles nodded. "I agree."

"Writing a nasty message on your garage door is a far cry from shooting into a crowd of people." He raked a hand through his salt-and-pepper hair as his blue eyes drilled his son. "There were three shots fired today. All of those were aimed at you."

"Yes, I noticed that."

Ryan pursed his lips as he listened to his father.

"I don't like it," Aiden continued. "I'm putting protection on you until we get this figured out. More protection than just a car sitting outside your house at night." He looked at Ryan. "Can you take care of that?"

"Consider it done."

Charles shifted and he grimaced. "People are going to accuse you of favoritism. Again."

"So be it. A car will be stationed outside your house 24/7. You'll have a tail and security at your office. One of your brothers will be around when they can."

"Dad," Charles protested. "You don't have the manpower for that. Not to mention the fact that it could be political suicide. The people in this town aren't convinced I'm not a murderer. For you to make this move...it might not be smart if you have plans to win the election."

Aiden's eyes hardened. "Your safety and the safety of my grandchildren are far more important than any political race." His eyes clouded. "It's the right thing to do and I'm going to do it."

Aiden glanced at Demi—and at her bandaged arm. "That protection will cover you, too. This guy doesn't seem to care who's in the path of his bullets."

"What about Douglas and Merry's wedding?" Charles asked. "I hate to let this guy keep me away.

Then again, I don't want to show up and lure him there, either."

Aiden drew in a deep breath. "I've already discussed this with Douglas and Merry. Bottom line is they want you there. Security will be tight not only because of what's going on with you, but because of Burke and his veiled threats."

"He's made threats?" Owen asked, eyes narrowing.

"Not blatant ones, no. But his nastiness just keeps getting worse as this election gets closer. He plays dirty. It wouldn't surprise me if Burke has some sort of agenda, a plan to use the wedding as a way to further his own political ambitions." Aiden waved a hand at Charles's questioning look. "How he could do that, I have no idea. I just want to cover every angle when it comes to making sure Merry and Douglas's day goes off without a hitch."

Charles's father pursed his lips. "The reception at Connolly's Catch is a private one. No one gets in without an invitation." He paused. "I'm even going to have a couple of guys on the roofs watching. No way is anything going to mess up this wedding." Then he gave a grim smile. "Actually with all the security at the wedding, you'll probably be safer there than at your house."

Charles's gave a slow nod and shot a glance at Demi. "Fine. We'll be there."

"It'll be the same setup for the rehearsal tonight."

Charles stood. "I'll be there for that, too, then."

Aiden walked them to the door. "Ryan, let's get that security detail going. Yesterday."

"Yes, sir."

As Ryan got on his phone, Charles looked at Owen. "Uh, Dad, could we have a word with you?"

Aiden paused and glanced between his sons. "What is it?"

Owen opened his mouth and shut it. Charles looked at Demi. "Do you mind waiting in the hall for a minute?"

She raised a brow. "Oh, sure." Once she left, the brothers turned back to their father and Charles tried again. "Dad, we came across a picture of—"

Aiden's phone rang the same time Owen's did and Charles clamped his lips on the words he'd been trying to force past clenched teeth.

"Excuse me, I need to take this." Aiden grabbed the phone, listened and said, "I've got to go. They've found some evidence on the shooter I need to look at."

"What kind of evidence?" Charles asked.

"I'll fill you in when I know." Aiden left and Charles felt a tide of frustration rush over him. As Owen listened to the person on the other end of his line, Charles went to find Demi standing in the hall, leaning against the wall.

His phone buzzed signaling a text message. He checked it then told Demi, "Victoria just sent me a text. She wants to know if she can keep the kids the rest of the day and bring them to the rehearsal tonight. Apparently Paige is having a good time reading to them. Why don't you take the rest of the day off? Enjoy some time to yourself." He glanced at the officer who'd been assigned to Demi. "Or with your shadow there. I'm going to be really busy with all of the pre-wedding stuff but I'll have someone come by to pick you up for the wedding tomorrow afternoon. It's at two o'clock."

"I guess that'll be all right. You don't need help with the children tonight?"

He shook his head. "They're in the wedding and I'll have enough family there to help me out if I need it." He touched her wounded arm. "Take the time. Rest. Do whatever it is you need to do."

Demi nodded. "All right."

"Great," Charles said. "I'll see you tomorrow at the wedding. I'll be saving a seat for you."

"Sure."

"Hold up, guys." Owen caught their attention and they turned as Owen said, "Thanks for the tip." He hung up and said, "We just got some info on Demi's identity."

Charles heard her indrawn breath and felt the sudden tremble in her hands. "Who was it?"

"A hotel clerk in Springfield. Apparently, he'd been visiting relatives here in Fitzgerald Bay and saw a clip of the news. He called it in yesterday. It took us this long to determine it's legit."

"So, he knows who I am?" The hope in her voice grabbed Charles and he found himself praying Owen said yes.

"No. Not really." Her hope deflated like a punctured balloon and Charles squeezed her fingers. "But he did recognize your picture. He said you'd been living at that hotel for about three weeks before you just disappeared without a word. You never checked out, you never claimed your things."

"My things?" she whispered. "I have things?"

Owen offered her a gentle, sympathetic smile. "Apparently. He said he had boxed them up in case something had happened to you and the police came asking questions."

"What else?"

"He said you registered under the name of Michelle Smith and always paid for the room daily. Never in advance. You were quiet, kept to yourself and seemed like a nice person."

"Michelle?"

"He didn't think it was your real name. He said he called you by that name twice and you never responded." He paused. "He also said you seemed like you were afraid all the time."

"Afraid? Of what?"

"That he didn't know."

Demi drew in a deep breath. "I need to go to that

hotel. I need to see it, see the room. Maybe that will trigger my memory."

"I agree," Charles said, "but you're not going alone. I'll go with you."

"When?"

He rubbed his chin. He knew she was anxious to get to that hotel. He didn't blame her. "I have the rehearsal dinner tonight and the wedding tomorrow."

"I hate to ask you to take me on Sunday."

Charles looked at his brother. "Why don't we call and see when he's going to be there?"

"Good idea," Owen said. He pulled out his phone. "I've got the number right here." He put the phone on speaker.

"Springfield Hotel."

"This is Detective Owen Fitzgerald in Fitzgerald Bay. I spoke with you earlier."

"Yes, sir."

"When would be a good time for us to come by and pick up Ms….uh…Smith's things?"

"I'm getting ready to leave in a few minutes to go out of town again for a funeral. I'll be back Monday morning."

"We'll see you then."

Owen hung up and Charles lifted a brow at Demi. "We'll go first thing Monday morning. Is that all right?"

He could see the longing on her face and felt terrible asking her to wait a few more days, but he couldn't leave yet—and he sure didn't want her going alone.

"I could go myself, take the bus," she said. "I really don't want to put anyone out."

"No!" Charles shouted the word and she blinked. He calmed his voice. "Sorry, but I don't think that's a good idea. You need someone with you." He pulled in a breath. "Just…please…let me go with you."

After what seemed like an eternity, she finally nodded. "Okay. I don't really want to go by myself anyway. I suppose waiting a couple more days won't hurt anything."

"Great."

The look of hopeful anticipation on her face caused mixed feelings and emotions to swirl through him. At first he couldn't figure out what was wrong, then realization hit him.

Once Demi discovered who she was, what if she didn't need—or want—him anymore?

FOURTEEN

Demi grabbed her light jacket from the closet and her keys from the kitchen counter. Hurrying from the apartment, she waved to the officer assigned to watch her. He stepped out of the cruiser. "Everything all right, ma'am?"

"Yes, I just decided I wanted to take a walk on the beach. Is that okay?"

Hesitation made the man pause before he said, "I think it should be. I'll follow behind you. As long as you're not out of my sight."

Demi thought about the numerous hiding places along the rocks near Charles's house. She thought about the shots that had been fired from the building overlooking the park. Would someone try to shoot at her if she went on the beach? But the person had been aiming at Charles, not her.

Squaring her shoulders, she determined the man wouldn't make her a prisoner in her own home. "I promise to stay within your sight. I just want to walk on the beach a little. Do some thinking."

"Come on, I'll give you a lift. It'll be safer than that bicycle."

She smiled. The whole town knew she didn't drive. Demi climbed in the cruiser and participated in the small talk until he pulled into the parking area with beach access. It was farther down from Charles's house, an area she hadn't yet explored. But she noticed the clear view of the beach. The officer wouldn't have any trouble keeping an eye on her. And she didn't plan to go far anyway.

Climbing out, she said, "Thanks. I won't be too long."

"Take your time."

Demi followed the path to the beach, noting she still felt like she was walking around with a big old target on her back. Although why someone would want to single her out to terrify, she couldn't fathom. The hotel clerk had said she'd seemed afraid, that she'd paid her bill daily. To her that sounded like someone who wasn't sure if she would be staying in the same place from one day to the next.

So was she running from someone?

Had she committed some crime and was running from the police? But her fingerprints hadn't turned up anything so she really didn't think she was a criminal.

Shuddering at the thought, lost in her thoughts, she almost didn't see the young woman until she was nearly upon her. It was the woman from the café, Olivia Henry's cousin, Meghan.

"Oh, hello."

"Hi." The tall woman with the hazel eyes and blond hair offered a cautious smile.

"Sorry, I was lost in my own world. How are you?"

"I'm fine." A pause. "How is the nanny job working out?"

"It's working out well, thanks."

"Oh." The woman fidgeted for a moment then asked, "Do you mind if I ask you a few questions?"

"No, I suppose that's fine. What kind of questions?"

"Don't you think it's possible that Charles killed her?"

Demi didn't even hesitate. "Absolutely not."

Meghan eyed her. "You sound very sure about that."

"He didn't do it. I know I've only known him for a few weeks, but I have no doubts about him on that particular issue."

Meghan nodded. "I appreciate that."

"But you don't believe me?"

The woman shrugged, a sad, grief-filled movement that made Demi's heart ache. "I don't know. I've watched him from afar, I've heard the townspeople talk about him, so I've gotten conflicting information."

"I suppose you're keeping up with the investigation?"

Meghan's jaw tightened. "Every step of the way."

On impulse, Demi reached out and took the woman's hand. "I'm so sorry for your loss, but it wasn't Charles who killed her."

Meghan squeezed her hand then dropped it with a sigh. "Thanks."

Then Meghan turned and walked back the way she'd come. Demi watched her go and prayed they would find Olivia's murderer before too much longer. Certainly before the person had the opportunity to kill again.

Charles paced the floor at the church. Last night the rehearsal had gone off without a hitch. Security ensured no one bothered the happy couple and his children were fully entertained by the other children involved in the wedding.

The whole process brought back memories of his own wedding. A lot of flash, a lot of money and very little substance if Kathleen could walk out on him and their children so easily. Her unfaithfulness was a sore spot that still chafed if he thought about it too long.

Which he'd been doing ever since finding the picture of his father with another woman. And a baby. His mistress and child out of wedlock?

Did he believe that?

Strangely enough, he did. Even with no concrete proof other than the picture and how close the couple stood, their expressions, the look in their eyes, Charles knew in his gut it was true.

His father had cheated on his mother.

The thought made his blood boil. Anger with his father wanted to surface, but Charles held it back. If he let it out, he'd cause friction at the wedding. And there was no way he was doing that. Especially without knowing for *certain* that it was true.

He and Owen would confront their father at the right time in the right way. And soon. After the wedding.

Right now, he kept an eye out for Demi, anxious to see her, to reassure himself that she was fine. Of course, if she wasn't fine, he would know about it, so he could relax. Right? At least that's what he told himself.

"Ready to do this thing?"

He looked up to see Ryan, Owen and his father standing in the door. Owen looked tense. He knew he was thinking about the photo. So was Charles. He kept his voice light. They had so many questions for Aiden. If he had an affair. Who the woman was. Did they have a half sibling? "I'm ready, but what about Douglas?"

"He's chomping at the bit," Aiden said. "Paige has your little ones under control for now. No guarantee on how long that'll last."

Charles laughed. "True." He looked at the gathering crowd. "Is Demi here?"

"Officer Bolton just delivered her safe and sound. She's sitting with the family."

Charles felt that weight slide from his shoulders. "Good, thanks."

"Now, let's go round up Douglas and get this thing done."

Within thirty minutes, Charles was standing up in front of the crowd, his eyes scanning, his senses alert. Even though he could see how tight security was, it didn't stop him from keeping a keen eye out for trouble. Every so often, his gaze would land on Demi and he'd feel a jolt in the vicinity of his heart.

Douglas and Merry had decided to place his mother's picture on the organ and Charles couldn't help staring at it, wondering if she ever knew her husband had been unfaithful. If she had, she'd obviously forgiven him and they'd worked through it. However, Charles felt his anger stir.

Forcing himself to pay attention to the service, he was relieved when the minister finally pronounced his brother lawfully wed and no one had disrupted the nuptials.

Breathing a sigh of relief, but not relaxing his guard, he felt the comfortable weight of the pistol in his shoulder holster. Until Olivia's murderer was caught, Charles wouldn't go anywhere without the weapon.

As the wedding party dispersed, Charles wondered what it would be like to be married to Demi. He could envision her in a white gown and—

Cutting off those thoughts for now, he promised himself he'd revisit them when the time was right.

As they waited for the photographer to set up his equipment, Charles motioned for Demi to stay. She nodded and settled back into the pew.

As soon as the pictures were finished, they would make their way to Connelly's Catch for the reception.

Finally, he saw his dad standing alone, taking in the merriment. The look on his father's face made Charles's gut burn with resentment. What right did he have to be so proud?

His eye caught Owen's. Owen's expression said he was thinking about the photo, as well. Charles leaned down and whispered in Demi's ear, "Excuse me a moment, will you?"

"Sure." Demi raised a brow as though to ask if everything was all right. He patted her shoulder to silently reassure her and she turned back to listen to Fiona.

He hadn't shared with her about the picture and what he and Owen suspected. He wouldn't until he had the truth from his father's lips.

He slipped up beside Owen. "Before or after the pictures?"

"After. No sense in ruining them for Douglas and Merry."

Another pause then Charles asked in a low voice, "What do you really think? Did Dad have an affair? A child with another woman? You saw the pictures."

In an equally soft tone, Owen said, "My gut says yes."

And then there was no more time for talk. Charles posed and smiled until his cheek muscles spasmed. Brianne and Aaron finally tired and protested loud enough that the photographer agreed he had enough pictures and they could all be dismissed.

Driving the short distance to Connolly's Catch, Charles kept an eye on the surrounding traffic. Demi teased Brianne and Aaron, and Charles struggled with what he would say to his father. How did one confront one's parent about his infidelity?

"Charles? Are you all right? You've been awfully quiet."

"I'm… I need to talk to my father about something unpleasant and I'm not looking forward to it."

She grimaced. "I'm sorry."

"Yeah." He forced a smile. "Come on, let's get something to eat, I'm starved."

They got the kids and made their way into the restaurant. Tantalizing smells made his stomach growl even more, although it was a bit early for supper.

Music played. Douglas and Merry danced a slow dance in the center of the dance floor. The lovesick look on his brother's face made Charles glance at

Demi. She took everything in, delight written in her eyes.

Soon, she might get her memory back. The question from the other day crossed his mind. As much as he wanted her to heal and know who she was, where would he fit in her life once she did? Disgusted with his selfishness, he forced the insecurity from his thoughts and caught Owen's eye.

Owen walked over, followed by Victoria. "What's going on?" she asked. "I saw that look you two exchanged."

"We're going to talk to Dad about that picture," Charles said.

Victoria frowned. "Let me see it again. I know I've seen it somewhere—" She broke off and paled.

Charles lasered in on her. "You remembered where you saw it."

She nodded, a slow nod that conveyed her reluctance to tell him what she was thinking. "Come on, Victoria. What is it?"

Her gaze darted to Charles's father who still stood apart from the festivities. "I'm pretty sure that's the picture Olivia gave me to hang on the wall in the café."

Charles felt his heart slam into his ribs. "Olivia? She has something to do with this?"

Another wide-eyed nod and a nervous glance at Aiden. "Olivia came into the café one day shortly before she died and handed me a copy of this picture. She asked me to hang it on the wall—"

At her pause, Owen pushed her. "Why?"

"To honor the memory of…her parents."

Charles froze. "Olivia's parents?"

"Yes," Victoria whispered.

Charles's gut churned. If what Victoria said was true, not only had Olivia been his nanny, she'd also been his half sister. He almost couldn't wrap his mind around it. One look at Owen's white face said his brother was having the same problem.

"I'm sorry," Victoria said, "but I'm absolutely positive that's what she said."

"And it's the same picture."

"Yes."

"Olivia knew," Charles muttered. "That's why she came to Fitzgerald Bay." He looked at Owen and Victoria. "She never said a word."

Owen ran a hand through his hair and drew in a ragged breath. "Unfortunately, if Dad knew who Olivia was—and I highly suspect he did—we now have another suspect in Olivia's murder."

"Let's go," Charles said.

The man was alone, still observing the crowd around him. Together, they approached. "Talk to you a minute?" Charles asked.

Aiden smiled. Then frowned as he discerned the seriousness of their expressions. "What is it?"

Owen simply reached into his pocket and pulled out the photo. "This."

Aiden looked at it. His face paled and Charles saw him swallow hard before he asked, "Where did you get this?"

"We found it in your tackle box the day we went to get that fishing rod for Demi."

Aiden swiped a hand across his lips and cleared his throat. "I see."

"Yeah," Charles said. "We see, too."

"Did you kill Olivia, Dad?" Owen asked in a low voice.

Their father jerked and choked. Shock made his pupils dilate. "What? No, I… No. How can you even ask that?"

"You certainly have motive." Charles kept his voice even while Owen pinched the bridge of his nose.

"Come with me," Aiden ordered, having regained some of his composure.

"Where?"

"Someplace private and we won't be overheard."

Demi watched Charles walk from the main part of the restaurant into a back room with his brother and father. They looked so serious she almost got up and followed, but decided it wasn't her business. Charles would fill her in when he could.

Leaning over, she said to Fiona, "I'm going to the ladies' room. I'll be right back."

"Sure."

Demi got up and made her way in the direction the sign pointed. As she walked, several people welcomed her. The small hall with the restrooms at the end was empty. Catching her breath, she started down toward the women's room and felt the hairs on the back of her neck lift.

Spinning, she saw no one.

But the feeling that someone was watching her was very strong. So strong she shivered.

Her eyes scanned the crowd beyond the hall and saw nothing that should concern her.

She turned back to enter the bathroom.

Then looked behind her once more.

A young man dressed in a pin-striped suit stood there watching her.

Demi pushed open the door to the bathroom and rushed inside. She let it close behind her, feeling her heart thump against her chest.

Who was he? Why was he watching her?

A noise in the stall behind her told her that she wasn't alone. Relief filled her and she took a deep breath as she washed her hands.

The occupant of the stall came out and smiled. "It was a beautiful wedding, wasn't it?"

"It sure was."

Demi decided to follow the woman out. She wanted the company.

As they left the ladies' room, Demi's heart slowed as she gazed on the empty hall.

As she and the woman in front of her passed a section of the hall that branched off, a hand reached out and grasped her upper arm.

A scream welled in her throat only to die a quick death when a voice asked, "Demi?"

Gasping, heart pounding, she spun to see the same young man who had watched her enter the restroom. He had stylishly messy dark hair and brown eyes. Hand over her heart, she said, "Yes?"

He held out his hands. "I'm sorry, I didn't mean to startle you."

"It's all right. Do I know you?"

He blinked and she saw the hurt in his eyes. "Well, I would hope so. I'm your fiancé."

FIFTEEN

Charles watched his father pace the small room. On the other side of the door, the merriment went on. Charles wanted to be out there, enjoying the party with his brother, but he wouldn't rest until his father said what he had to say.

Aiden rubbed his eyes. "Okay, so you found the picture and put two and two together. That was twenty-three years ago."

"Yeah. So?"

"So, your mother and I had hit a rough patch. We'd agreed to a divorce. I thought that my marriage was over. I was lonely, grieving…" He stopped and shut his eyes while letting out a blustery sigh. "I made a mistake," he admitted in a low voice. "I was wrong. Horribly, irrevocably wrong. When Tara called to tell me she was pregnant, I was already back and working things out with your mother. But…I just couldn't leave Tara with nothing. I flew back to Ireland to make sure she and the baby were well taken care of."

"Did Mom know?"

Aiden swallowed. "No. I never told her."

Charles nodded. At least she was spared that.

"So, Olivia Henry was your daughter."

A heavy sigh. "Yes. And I see your point about motive. Trust me, I've thought about how all this looks, but I didn't kill her." He looked at Charles. "And I know you didn't, either."

"The rest of the family needs to know this."

"Why?"

Charles looked at his father, incredulous that the man had to ask. "Because, it's going to come out one way or another. Olivia's dead," he hissed. "You can't keep your relationship to her a secret much longer. It would be much better for everyone coming from you than to see it on the news."

Aiden paced from one end of the room to the other. He finally stopped in front of Charles and Owen. "Okay. You're right." His gaze hardened. "But I tell them in my own way, my own time. Let's see if we can get Olivia's murder solved before we drop this bomb on them."

Charles glanced at Owen who gave a reluctant nod. "Fine."

Owen stared at his father. "Those baby items that were sent to the station anonymously last month. You sent those, didn't you?"

Charles remembered Owen talking about receiving several baby items, including a baby's hospital bracelet, a receiving blanket and an uncashed check for ten thousand dollars made out to Olivia Henry. These items had led Owen and Ryan to the conclusion that Olivia had a baby somewhere.

And their father knew it.

Charles felt sick.

"Yes, I did. Olivia gave them to me. After she was murdered, I felt terrible and knew I couldn't just sit on that evidence." He paused. "Nor could I come forward and tell everything I knew. That seemed like the right thing to do at the time."

"The right thing—" Charles broke off and ground his teeth. Did his father even understand how that sounded? "The right thing?" Charles felt all the rage he'd been holding in ever since being considered a suspect and then finding that picture in Dad's tackle box come boiling to the surface. "The right thing would have been to walk away from a woman who wasn't your wife twenty-three years ago. If you'd done the *right thing* twenty-three years ago, we wouldn't be in this situation, would we?"

Owen stepped between him and his father who'd clenched his fists. Charles stepped away, appalled at how close he was to losing control. Drawing in a deep breath, he closed his eyes and turned his back to Owen and his dad.

Aiden's voice, gravelly with regret, said, "You're right. Everything you said is right. I'm sorry, son, and I'll make it right. I will."

"When?" Charles demanded.

His father glanced at Douglas and Merry. "I'll tell everyone at the next Sunday family dinner. Douglas and Merry don't need to know until they get back from their honeymoon. Agreed?"

Charles and Owen nodded. "Agreed," Charles muttered.

Demi stared at the unknown man in front of her. At a loss for words, she simply gaped.

He gave a self-conscious laugh. "Um…so, are you okay? I saw your picture on the news and couldn't believe it was you. I mean, I have so much I want to talk to you about."

She felt frozen, the man in front of her a stranger. And yet, her fiancé? How could this be?

Gulping, she finally found her voice. "I…I'm sorry. I don't know who you are. I have amnesia. What's your name?"

"I'm Alan Gregor, Demi. Come on. Amnesia? Really?"

"Is there a problem?" Charles's voice cut through her brain fog.

Whirling, she stared into his blue eyes. Eyes she'd come to love over such a short period of time. Not just his eyes, but everything about him.

Only she didn't have the right to love him. She'd already promised her love to another.

Grief nearly shattered her. She should be rejoicing that someone had finally come forward, but she couldn't get past the fact that she was going to lose Charles. And the children. And his crazy beloved family.

"I…" What could she say?

"Demi?" A hard hand gave her shoulder a gentle shake.

"Charles, this is…" A sob nearly broke through. Clearing her throat, she tried again. "This is Alan Gregor. He claims that he's my fiancé."

"Your what?" His face paled and she saw him swallow hard.

She drew in a shuddering breath. "He says he's my fiancé. But I don't remember him." Her voice shook. Charles looked like he'd been dealt a blow to his solar plexus.

She looked at Alan and bit her lip. "I'm sorry, I don't remember you."

Over his shoulder, she spotted Owen, a thundercloud on his face. Ryan and their father were right behind him. For a brief moment, Demi put aside the strange man who'd just rocked her world once again and focused on the approaching family. "Charles? I think something's wrong." She pointed.

He turned and immediately went tense. "What is it?" he asked his tight-lipped father. "What's wrong now?"

Aiden said, "Burke Hennessy's dead."

Charles froze. "Dead?"

"A heart attack is what it looks like," Aiden

growled. "They'll do an emergency autopsy. We should have the report sometime tomorrow."

"Oh, no," Demi whispered. "Poor Christina."

"Yes." Aiden nodded. "She's the one who found him. Walked in and started screaming according to her nanny. The nanny called 9-1-1. It's a shame. I mean, I didn't care much for the guy, but I didn't wish him dead." A pause. He looked at his sons. "The media's already all over this." Aiden zoomed in on Charles. "Word's already filtering down that the death is being covered up as a heart attack. They're speculating that you had something to do with it."

Charles flinched. "What? Why? How did they come up with that ridiculous idea?"

Ryan rubbed his eyes. "Someone said they overheard you threaten Burke."

"I never threatened the man," Charles ground out. "I told him to buzz off and stay out of my business, but I never threatened him."

"Well, you were here surrounded by witnesses when he died so I think it'll be easy enough to prove you didn't have anything to do with it." Aiden gestured toward a wide-eyed Alan. "Who's this?"

Alan held out a hand. "I'm Alan Gregor, Demi's fiancé."

In a dazed voice, Demi told what Alan had explained to her only moments before.

"How did you get in here?" Charles asked. "This reception was by invitation only."

"I…sort of lifted an invitation." He pulled it out of his pocket and waved it with a sheepish look.

Aiden nearly growled. "You had no business doing that. I should have you thrown out."

"I'm sorry, it's just that I was trying to find a way to talk to Demi, but she's surrounded by cops all the time and I…" He shrugged and looked down. "I'm sorry. I should have found another way."

"Yeah, you should have. What took you so long to come forward?" Charles asked.

Alan winced. "It's a long story."

"Why don't we all find a seat and you can fill us in," Charles murmured. Already he didn't like the guy. Demi looked like she'd been sucker punched. The white lines around her lips and eyes betrayed her tension.

"Ah, do you mind if I speak to Demi alone?"

The panic in her eyes was all the answer Charles needed. "Actually, I do mind. We've come to think of Demi as family, so until you check out, I'll just stick around. Unless Demi wants me to leave…."

"No, stay. Please."

The grateful look she shot him told him that his answer was the right one.

A flash of anger on Alan's face, quickly snuffed, made Charles a little wary. Then again, he supposed could understand it, too. If he'd just found his fiancée and another man was horning in…well, he wouldn't like it, either.

But it didn't stop him from following the two of them over to an empty table. The reception was winding down. Douglas and Merry would soon leave and Charles wanted to wish them well.

With one eye on the newlyweds, he focused the rest of his attention on Alan and Demi.

Alan cleared his throat and leaned in so he could be heard over the music.

"I didn't come sooner because I've been out of the country."

"What's my name?" Demi asked.

"Demetria Michelle Townsend."

He saw her lips move as she repeated the name. Then she whispered, "I was right. I remembered my name." She smiled, tears glittering in her eyes.

"Do you remember anything about what happened?" Alan asked.

"No. The police think I was attacked and left for dead. I was in the hospital after I was found for about three weeks. When I woke up, I had no memory of anything except my first name."

"Oh, Demi, honey," Alan murmured as he reached over and grasped her fingers for a squeeze. Demi pulled away before Charles had to smash the man's nose.

Lord, Charles began to pray, *I know I've been distant since Kathleen left me and that was wrong. I know I want to pray a selfish prayer and beg You to get this guy away from her, but if that's not in*

Your plan, then I ask that You help me accept and deal with it because there's no way I can do that on my own strength.

"…right, Charles?" Demi asked.

He blinked. "I'm sorry, I was thinking about something. What?"

"I said you planned to take me to the hotel where I was staying before I was attacked, but now that Alan is here, that might not be necessary." She frowned. "Although I do want to get my things."

"What hotel?" Alan asked.

So Demi explained that part of her story while Charles fumed.

Charles looked at Alan. "The clerk said she seemed afraid. Do you have any idea what she would have been afraid of?"

Alan's eyes went wide. "No, I'm sorry, I can't imagine." He looked at Demi. "In all your letters that you wrote, you never said anything about being afraid."

"Letters?"

Alan smiled. "Letters, cards, emails. You were so diligent in making sure I had a huge number of them." His eyes lowered and he cleared his throat as though his emotions were too much. "I don't know what I would have done without you, Demi."

The hoarse words rocked Charles back on his heels. He knew exactly how the man felt. While in the service, letters and cards from family and friends had kept him going. What would Charles do if Demi left him? Chose Alan over him? A coldness swept over him as he considered the possibility. Then he firmed his jaw. No way. He wouldn't let that happen.

But how could he stop it? *God, please, do something...*

"Tell us your story, Alan," Charles said.

Alan sighed and rubbed his eyes. "Right. Okay. I was a government contractor working over in Iraq when my colleagues and I were hit with an IED."

At Demi's blank look, Charles said, "Improvised Explosive Device. A roadside bomb. Generally homemade and designed to do as much damage as possible."

"Oh," she gasped. "I'm so sorry."

Alan shrugged, but the lines on his face said the memory wasn't pleasant. Again, Charles could relate. He didn't like that. He didn't want to feel anything but dislike for the man who wanted to take Demi away from him.

The man continued. "I was the only survivor. It took me weeks to recover. When I did, I tried to contact you, but got nowhere. I was sent home on medical leave and started searching for you. Just as I was about to go to the cops, I saw your picture on the news and saw that you'd been attacked in an attempted robbery. But no one told me that you had amnesia, not even the nurses I talked to at the hospital. They just said you caught a bus to someplace near the coast. It took forever to track you down."

Demi simply stared at Alan. Charles couldn't read her expression and that bothered him.

Alan said, "I couldn't understand why you hadn't contacted me, why the letters suddenly stopped. Why you weren't answering your phone." He shrugged and a sad smiled pulled at his lips. "Now I understand." He looked around the room, at Charles then back at Demi. "I know you've made new friends, have a new life here, but I'm hoping you'll at least give me a chance, get to know me again."

Demi stood abruptly. "I need some air."

Demi didn't know whether to run or laugh or cry. Finally, she had what she'd been hoping—praying—for. Someone who knew her. Knew about her. And what did she do?

Run away.

But she needed time, space, to deal with this. To wrap her mind around everything.

She hadn't even asked about her family.

"Are you all right?"

Demi spun at the sound of the voice. It was the officer who'd been keeping an eye on her. Clearing her throat, she said, "Yes, I just need some time."

"Sure." He backed up, but she noticed he didn't leave her alone.

"Demi?"

She turned.

Charles. Tears welled as his warm hands settled on her shoulders. She felt his lips brush the edge of her hairline. "It'll be okay," he whispered.

Looking beyond him, she saw Alan standing in the doorway, watching, hands shoved in his pockets, mouth tight, brow furrowed. She moved away from Charles. "I'm going home. Give my best to Douglas and Merry for me. I'm sorry," she stammered, "I just need to be alone for a while."

She could see Charles wanted to argue—or at least go with her. But she turned on her heel, putting her back to him and Alan.

The officer followed at a discreet distance.

Demi's mind whirled. She needed guidance, direction. But all her friends were related to Charles. Who could she talk to? Who would be objective about her situation?

"Demi, wait!"

Turning, eyes nearly blinded with her tears, she made out Alan's form coming toward her. The officer followed behind.

"Demi." He caught up with her. "Please. Don't go yet. Come sit with me. Talk to me."

She wanted to. Only because she had a zillion questions to ask him. She searched for Charles, but he'd already left. That made her feel sad—and grateful. He'd been willing to honor her request for time alone.

And then there was Alan. Who seemed so desperate to be with her. She couldn't begrudge him that. How would she feel if the roles were reversed?

Brushing aside her tears and telling herself to grow a spine, she straightened her shoulders and nodded. "Fine. Let's go to the café, okay?"

"Sure."

Demi led the way, her heart beating double time once again. With everything in her, she wished Charles was beside her, but knew that wasn't fair to him or the man who'd just shown up in her life.

They found a table and ordered coffee. Thank goodness Victoria was still at the wedding reception. Demi didn't need her watchful eye.

As it was, nervous jitters made her hands shake. She took a sip of the steaming brew and said, "Can you please tell me a little about my family? My parents? Brothers and sisters?"

He hesitated, then said, "You're an only child. Your parents are missionaries in…ah…Brazil, I think you said. You can go months without hearing from them."

So that was why no one had reported her missing!

"But what about friends? A church family?"

He shrugged. "You lived with your parents in Brazil but came home to take care of their house. That's how we met. I leased the house next door to your parents. I asked you to stay a little longer rather than return to the mission field so that we could continue to grow our relationship." His eyes softened and his hand reached out to touch hers. "We fell in love and when I asked you to marry me, you said yes. That's about it."

Her head began to ache the way it did when she tried to think too hard, or when she tried to force the memories. This time she ignored it. "My parents' house," she said softly. "Where is it?"

"In Springfield."

"Where I was found. Where I stayed in the hospital."

"Yes."

"And yet no one knew who I was?"

"No, I guess not," he said slowly. "But it makes sense. You told me you fell in love with Brazil and hadn't been back to the States for a few years although you said your parents came back pretty regularly."

"I was a missionary?" The thought just registered. No wonder she'd been compelled to seek out God. Warmth infused her. She believed in God.

"Yes. You taught school."

"I'm a teacher."

"A missionary teacher."

Visions of children swam through her mind. Dark faces, dark eyes, smiles. Then yelling, a hard fist and a scream. She gasped.

Alan's grip tightened on her fingers. "You remember something."

"Ah, no. Yes. I'm not sure." She blinked the images away and the headache faded.

"Come with me."

"What?"

"Let me take you home. Show you where you live, where we were going to live after we were married."

The excitement in his voice made her hesitate. She didn't want to go with him. She wanted to go with Charles.

Something in her expression must have registered with him. "It's him, isn't it?"

Demi didn't bother to ask what he meant. "I'm not going to lie to you. I've developed feelings for Charles." His eyes shuttered and his lips tightened. "But," she hurried on to reassure him, "I want to be fair to you, too. I... Oh, my, I think I just need some time."

He smiled. A forced smile, but at least he was trying. "All right, Demi, just don't make any hasty decisions without letting me know. Please?"

"I think that's a reasonable request. I can do that," she promised.

"Good. Good."

Demi stood. "I'm going to lie down. I need to process all of this."

SIXTEEN

Charles slept little and when he woke Sunday morning, he was in a foul mood. Not only because he'd had almost no sleep, but because it was now 5:00 a.m. and he was wide awake. The twins still slept so he prowled the house on silent feet.

In the den, his eyes landed on his mother's Bible. The book held a prominent position on the mantel. His mother had given the Bible to him several weeks before she'd died, making him promise to live by it.

Regret pierced him. He'd read that book every day after her death, seeking solace and comfort in the word. But after Kathleen had left him, he'd lost the will, the energy, to do anything but get through each day only to fall into bed every night exhausted beyond belief.

Now, he pulled the Bible from its resting place. With a puff of his breath, he blew the layer of dust from the top.

Carrying the book to the recliner, he settled himself in the chair and opened the Bible. His mother's handwriting leaped off the pages. She'd taken copious notes over the years. His finger traced the words and wondered what she would have done, how she would have felt, had she known of her husband's infidelity.

She would have been hurt, betrayed, angry. Of course she would have felt all those emotions.

Would she have eventually forgiven? Probably.

Charles tried to find it in his heart to pray for Kathleen. To completely forgive her for deserting him and their children. To his surprise, the raging bitterness was gone, replaced by a sadness for the woman. A regret that he wasn't what she'd needed.

But a thankfulness that Demi had come along when she had.

His phone buzzed.

Owen had sent him a text: Call when you get up. Have news re: Burke's autopsy.

Charles lifted a brow. That was fast. His father must have pulled a few strings to get that done in such a short amount of time.

He punched in Owen's speed dial number.

Owen picked up on the second ring. "It was murder."

"How?"

"Apparently the man liked to drink at night. Someone slipped a lethal cocktail of prescription drugs in his drink."

"How do you know it wasn't suicide?"

"The ME found a feather in his throat."

"A feather?"

"As in from a feather pillow. Looks like someone doped him up good, then held a pillow over his face to make sure the deed was done."

"Wow."

"At least that's the speculation at this point. Tox screen was off the charts with all kinds of different drugs. I can't even remember the ones the ME listed."

Charles heard the weariness in his brother's voice. "You know we—the family, I mean—will be suspects, don't you?"

"Of course I know that," Owen snorted. "I've already thought about that. I can just see the headlines now. 'Fitzgerald family poisons rival for mayor.'"

"I don't suppose there's any way to keep this from the media."

"Not a chance."

"Right." Charles glanced at the clock on the wall. "I'm still planning on taking Demi to the hotel. She wants to get her things."

"And it's an opportunity to spend some time with her, eh?"

Charles felt the flush start at the base of his throat. Glad he was on the phone and not facing his brother, he simply said, "Yes."

Silence.

Then Owen said, "You're worried about this guy, Alan, aren't you?"

"I am."

"I don't envy your position," Owen said. "Let me know if you need my help with anything."

Charles didn't hesitate. "I want a background check on this guy."

"Absolutely. Consider it done." His brother paused. "One more thing. We've decided to release a picture of the dolphin charm found near Olivia's body to the media. Let them show it on the news and see if anyone can ID it. We've kind of sat on this piece of evidence because we were trying to track down where it came from without alerting the killer that we had it. We're hoping the killer doesn't even realize it's missing. However, we're running out of options and leads on this case and feel like it's time to reveal it and see what happens."

Charles drew in a deep breath. "Keep me updated."

"Will do."

Charles hung up and wondered if life would ever get back to normal.

After church Sunday, Demi and the Fitzgerald clan gathered at the ball field. Aiden had ordered extra security for the game just to be on the safe side. He'd thought about calling it off, but Charles said he would come up against such opposition that he'd relented.

With conditions.

There would be guards around the perimeter, and fans would have to consent to bag searches.

It looked like the entire town turned out for this special fundraiser game to benefit the children's hospital. Charles pushed the twins in the stroller and Demi walked beside them, her heart warm from being with them. She tried not to think about how much she liked being a part of this family. Because she had no assurance it would last.

At the bleachers, she joined Charles on the bottom one so the twins could be kept in their stroller as long as they would consent to it.

Paige and Victoria sat behind them.

"I'll play with them if you want me to, Uncle Charles," Paige offered.

Fiona's son, Sean, darted past followed by a group of his buddies.

Charles looked at Paige and smiled. "Maybe in a little while. They're pretty happy right now."

"Okay."

And then she saw something that disturbed her.

Alan Gregor sitting on the next set of bleachers, turned so he could see her.

When she caught his eye, he smiled and waved her over.

Her heart hit her toes. She didn't want to see Alan today.

The thought sent guilt coursing through her and she forced a smile. "Charles, I'm going to say hello to Alan."

The instant frown on his face sent a new surge of guilt. Guilt for...just being her and the uncertainty she'd brought into his life.

Biting her lip against the desire to ignore Alan and run back to her apartment—so she didn't have to deal with the stress of Alan's presence and Charles's unhappiness at the whole situation—she made her way over to the man who'd rocked her world yesterday and said, "Hi, Alan."

Delight lit his expression. "Demi. I knew you'd be here. Would you sit with me?"

Awkwardness hit her. "Well, I've come with Charles and the kids, so I guess I'll stay with them. But thank you."

Alan's shoulders drooped and he turned his head for a minute. Then he looked back at her. "Sure, sure. I understand." But she saw disappointment in his eyes and almost asked him if he wanted to join them. Then bit her tongue. She wouldn't do that to Charles.

And yet, Alan looked so sad. She said, "But I'd love to meet you after and get a cup of coffee or something. Maybe we could pick up our conversation and you could tell me a little more about—my life."

His shoulders straightened a bit and he smiled. "Sure, I'd love to do that."

Demi nodded and turned to catch Charles, his eyes questioning and shadowed. She swallowed hard and felt tears threaten.

What was she doing?

Keeping a tight rein on her emotions, she felt them testing her control.

Instead of walking back to Charles and the children, she turned left and headed for the building that held the restrooms.

She darted around the side and let the dam break.

Tears trickled down her cheeks and she leaned her head against the rough brick. *God, help me, what am I going to do? What is Your will in this?*

She had no ready answer for her desperate plea.

A hand fell on her shoulder and she turned to find Charles standing there, compassion written on his face. "Ah, Demi, I'm sorry."

She wrapped her arms around his waist and buried her nose in his chest. "Oh, Charles, I don't know what to do. I don't want to have coffee with him. I don't love him. I…I want to be with you, to keep building whatever it is we're building with each other and selfishly, maybe, I'm not ready to give that up."

Charles froze and she wished she could bite her tongue off. Why, oh why, had she blurted that out?

Heat scalded her cheeks and she didn't dare lift her head from his chest.

But he didn't give her a choice. His hand came up and he tucked a finger under her chin. Slowly, she gazed into his eyes.

He licked his lips then said, "I want that, too, Demi. I'm just not sure what to do about it."

Demi gave an anguished, humorless laugh as her embarrassment faded in the wake of his confession. "We can't do anything about it right now. Not until I figure out what to do about Alan, not until something gives with my memories."

"And not until I'm cleared of Olivia's murder."

Demi settled her forehead back against his shoulder. "This is all so crazy. When will it end?"

"Soon, I hope. Soon."

"Everything all right?"

Demi jerked at the woman's voice. Turning, she saw a uniformed officer standing, watching them. "We're fine," Demi said. "Just getting ready to go watch a softball game."

They walked back to the bleachers where Victoria had Brianne sitting in her lap. Paige sat in the dirt with Aaron as they ran his Matchbox cars through a maze Paige had drawn. Dino sat in the middle.

Demi's heart clenched. What would she do without this little family?

She felt Alan's gaze on her.

Glancing at him, she did her best to smile.

But shivered when he didn't smile back.

SEVENTEEN

Demi listened as Owen and Charles went back and forth about the trip to the Springfield Hotel. They'd decided to wait until after Burke Hennessy's funeral, which would be in less than two hours. The medical examiner had released the body, declaring all the evidence the police needed had been gathered.

Owen said, "After the funeral, I think I'll have an officer follow you."

Charles hesitated. "Why? Burke's dead."

Owen lifted a brow. "Burke wasn't the one shooting at you during the debate."

"True," Charles said. "Very true. So he either hired someone or it wasn't Burke."

"Exactly why we don't need to take any chances. Why don't you take Ryan with you?"

"Ryan?"

"He's a cop. He has the time. With the attempts on your life, I think it's the safe way to go."

Charles thought about it. "I've got my weapon."

"Yeah, but if you shoot him, you don't have to do the paperwork."

Charles smiled at Owen's attempt to lighten the mood. "Good point. All right, see if Ryan can go with us. Couldn't hurt to have him along."

"Good." Charles could hear the relief in Owen's voice.

"Thanks, Owen."

"Just stay out of trouble or I'll never hear the end of it from Ryan."

Demi saw Charles's truck pull up outside of The Reading Nook. Hurrying down the stairs, she couldn't quell the anxiety churning in her stomach. Today after the funeral, she would hold in her hands things that belonged to her. She was one step closer to finding out who she was. True, she now had a name, but she wanted her memories back.

Hopefully, a visit to the hotel she'd stayed in before the attack would offer that.

And then possibly, a visit to her home.

Her home. What was it like? Would she see pictures of her family, friends? Maybe the school where she taught.

And she would get to spend the day with Charles even if it included a funeral.

She climbed in the passenger seat and Charles said, "I appreciate you going with me."

"I didn't really know Burke very well, but I don't mind going."

"I feel like a hypocrite."

"Why? Because you couldn't stand the man and you're going to his funeral?"

Charles gave a short humorless laugh. "Exactly."

"Then why are you going?"

He let out a long sigh. "Because it's the right thing to do. The man had his issues and I think his wife, Christina, is going to need all the support she can get. She won't want it from us now, but maybe later, she'll realize…"

Demi took his hand and squeezed. "You're a very kind man, aren't you?"

He flushed. "I try." He paused. "I have to admit I'm hesitant to show up. I know Dad wants me to go, but I'm not sure that's the wisest decision he's made considering Burke's animosity toward our family." He shook his head as he made a left turn to head for the church.

Upon their arrival, the parking lot was almost full. In spite of Burke's attitude toward the Fitzgeralds, he was a popular man in town. Everyone who was anyone in Fitzgerald Bay had come to pay their respects.

Demi looked around and couldn't help but wonder if the person who'd killed Olivia was nearby. She spotted Meghan Henry and waved. Meghan waved back, but frowned when she saw who Demi was with.

Demi felt her heart dip at the response, but there was nothing she could do about it. Only by the authorities catching the real killer and clearing Charles's name would everyone finally see their concerns and suspicions had been wrong.

She prayed that happened soon.

"That was kind of Mrs. Mulrooney to offer to keep the children for you," she said to break the silence.

He smiled, a pulling of his lips that didn't quite reach his eyes. "She's a great lady."

Charles made the appropriate response, but Demi could see his attention was on the people going into the church. He caught her arm. "Do you mind if we go in toward the end?"

"You want to sit in the back?"

"If you don't mind."

"Not at all."

As they waited, Demi watched the crowd. Several people noticed her and Charles standing there and she saw them make comments. She felt Charles tense and was glad neither of them could hear what was being said.

"Are you ready?"

"Whenever you are."

He took her hand and led her to the door. As they

entered, she could see a few of the Fitzgeralds already seated. "You don't want to sit with your family?"

He shook his head. "I want to be able to see who's here."

Demi nodded and they found a seat in the back. She saw Aiden's salt-and-pepper head held high. Ryan and Owen flanked their father. Seated next to Owen was Paige then Victoria, Keira and Fiona.

Demi glanced toward the door and gasped as she recognized Alan. Charles leaned over. "What is it?"

"Why is he here?" she whispered.

Again, she felt him tense. "I don't know. Do you want me to ask him?"

Alan finally spotted her and made his way toward her. She gulped and shivered. What was it about him that made her uneasy?

She didn't have time to try and figure it out. Alan soon stood in front of her. He nodded to Charles, but didn't take his eyes off Demi. She asked, "What are you doing here, Alan? You didn't know Burke."

He shifted side to side for a moment then shoved his hands into the front pockets of his khaki slacks. "I know. But…I knew you'd be here."

Demi sighed. "Oh, Alan. Let's get through the funeral, all right?"

"Do you mind if I sit with you?"

"Sure." She looked at Charles who didn't look happy, but shrugged. They found their seats with Demi between the men. The tension surrounding them was thick; it had to be visible to anyone who looked at them.

The funeral lasted about an hour. A very long hour where Demi had to consciously remind herself not to squirm.

When it finally ended, Alan turned to her. "Could we go somewhere and talk?"

Demi bit her lip. "I'm sorry, Alan, we're going to take a little road trip. Another time, all right?"

"Oh, right. Sure." He gave them a tight smile and left through the side door.

Demi felt the tension ease as she looked at Charles. "I'm sorry about all this. All I want right now is to just to be sure about who I am."

He placed an arm over her shoulders. "Don't be sorry." She shivered at the intensity of his gaze. "But I'll tell you this. Even if you never remember anything, I already know who you are. You're beautiful and sweet with an open loving nature that's not easy to find. You have a strength in you that I don't think even you fully understand. But I see it and I admire you. Very much."

Her heart tripped over itself at his gentle words. "Thanks," she whispered.

"Anytime."

Demi's excitement knew no limits as she and Charles walked to his truck. There, they found Ryan leaning against the vehicle. When he saw them, he climbed into the back. Before he shut the door, Demi asked, "You're going with us?"

Charles said, "In light of everything going on, we thought it might be best."

In other words, they were afraid someone would follow them. She gulped. "Okay." Climbing into the front seat, some of her excitement faded.

But not all of it.

Buckling her seat belt, she turned to Charles. "Thanks for doing this."

He smiled at her. "No problem."

Ryan's phone rang and he talked in a low voice. She heard something about a background check. Demi said to Charles, "Alan offered to take me. I...I didn't want him to."

Charles put the truck in gear and she felt his eyes on her for a brief moment before he said, "I'm glad."

"I wanted to be with you," she almost whispered.

"And you feel guilty because of that?"

Demi looked out her window and nodded. "Is that wrong?" she asked turning to look at him once again.

Charles sighed. "No, I don't think so. And not necessarily because you just want to be with me, although I'd like to think that's why." His wink made her flush but she couldn't help the smile. And felt grateful for it. Charles continued, "But you know me. You're comfortable with me. Alan? You don't know anything about him. Why would you want a complete stranger sharing what's bound to be an emotional experience?"

Demi thought about that for a moment. She had to admit he was right. But she also silently admitted that she wanted to be with him and not Alan because she was in love with Charles. Not Alan.

But apparently she'd loved Alan at one time. Hadn't she?

Confusion and frustration swirled. She'd wanted to know who she was. Now she wasn't so sure she could handle everything that knowledge came with.

Instead of blurting out her feelings with Ryan in the back, she simply said, "That's true."

The rest of the drive was made in silence broken only by Ryan's phone calls.

He finally hung up just as they pulled into the hotel parking lot.

Demi glanced around praying for a spark of a memory. It was a nondescript place, nothing fancy, but not a dump, either.

"Let's go see the clerk," Charles said.

Climbing out of the truck, Demi continued to push her brain. She had a flash, a different one this time. Of running down a dark alley, looking back over her shoulder. She could feel the terror spiking through her and she gasped.

Charles turned and gripped her hand. "Are you all right?"

"Just a memory, I think. I was scared and running from something."

He and Ryan exchanged a look. Together, Charles still holding her hand, they walked into the hotel. The empty lobby echoed their arrival.

The clerk looked up and smiled. "Hi, I'm Martin Fields. You the folks I'm expecting?"

"We are," Charles said as he shook the man's hand.

The clerk's eyes landed on Demi. "Sure, I remember you. Ms. Smith, right?"

"Actually, it's Townsend, but I guess I was registered under Smith."

Confusion flickered, but she felt quite sure it wasn't the first weird story he'd heard. Mr. Fields said, "I'll just get your things."

He disappeared into the back and when he returned, he was holding a laundry basket full of neatly folded clothes. A large cardboard box sat on top of the clothes.

Carrying both items to the dining area to the left of the lobby, he set it down on one of the tables. "You didn't have much and I'm not exactly sure why I kept it, but maybe it was the Lord's leading."

Demi smiled. "I'm sure it was."

Anxiety gripped her. She inspected the laundry. Lifted a blue cotton dress from the top and shook it out. A memory flashed, but it was gone before she could grasp it. Another dress stared up at her. She set the first dress aside and ran her hands over the flower print on the second dress.

"Demi?" Charles's voice reached her through the fog of her scattered thoughts. "Are you okay?"

"I wore this when I flew home," she whispered. "You remember?"

"Not really...." She bit her lip. "And yet, I do. I remember hugging someone, a woman, in the airport. Then being on a plane." She frowned. "But it's so vague, just bits and pieces. Snatches here and there."

"That's more than you had just a little while ago."

"True." She looked in the cardboard box and pulled out a framed photograph. The woman wore a floppy hat and a long button up shirt. She had weathered skin and a big smile. The man beside her wore khaki shorts and a blue T-shirt. "My parents."

She knew it without question. And felt a longing to see them. Then wrap her arms around them.

A tear slipped down her cheek and she brushed it away.

Charles's comforting presence behind her gave her the strength to pull out the other items. A few toiletries, another picture with her, a young man in his early twenties. Who was he? A friend? A cousin? A brother?

She frowned and went through the rest of the pictures. Biting her lip, she looked up at the men. "I don't have a picture of Alan."

"You don't?" Charles leaned closer.

"No. I wonder why."

"Maybe you had it on you when you were attacked," Ryan suggested.

"Maybe." She opened a small bag and pulled out a small card. "My driver's license!"

Looking at it, she read the address. "Forty-five Lenox Lane."

"That's about twenty minutes from here," the clerk said.

When Charles lifted a brow at him, he shrugged. "I recognize that street. I used to drive a FedEx truck before getting into the hotel business a year ago."

"I want to go home." As soon as she said the words, the fear hit her. She began to shake.

"Demi?" Ryan asked.

Charles gripped her fingers. "What is it?"

"I can't go home. It's not safe there," she blurted out.

Charles looked at Ryan. "How far from her home was she found?"

Ryan pulled out his iPhone and looked it up. "About thirty minutes in the opposite direction from where we are."

The sliding glass door of the hotel shattered inward, spraying them all.

EIGHTEEN

More bullets peppered the area, and Charles felt his back sting. Had he been shot? No, he'd been shot before and this didn't feel like that.

Without stopping to think, he grabbed Demi and pulled her to the floor. Ryan tackled the clerk. Charles was only seconds behind Ryan in drawing his weapon and heading in the direction from where the shots had come.

He saw a flash from the parking garage across the street and another bullet slammed into the floor in front of him. He ducked and rolled.

"Stay here!" Charles yelled over his shoulder at Demi and the clerk. Not waiting to see if they obeyed him, he and Ryan reached the inside of the first set of sliding glass doors and huddled in the corner. He wasn't sure the shooter was finished.

Ryan copied him on the opposite side.

Warm outside air rushed over Charles, blowing in through the gaping hole in the second set of glass doors. On the street pedestrians cowered behind whatever shelter they could find. Screams still echoed.

"Stay down!" Ryan shouted. "Stay down!"

Someone had followed them. The thought made Charles's gut churn. They'd been careful, took a winding route, watched their backs. How had they been followed?

And the guy shot into a hotel? Why? That was crazy, wasn't it? What were the odds of hitting a target shooting through two sets of glass doors?

The question puzzled him. But one thing was certain.

Whoever was after him was determined to rub him out of the picture.

But not if Charles found him first. His jaw felt tight enough to shatter. He looked toward the parking garage again. To Ryan, he said, "He's using a high-powered rifle and he's on the third floor of that garage. I'm going after him."

"No, you're not."

Charles glared at Ryan. He wasn't the law in this city, but he was still his brother. "I have to."

Ryan shook his head. "We need to wait for backup."

"By then he'll be gone. This has to end now."

Charles took off for the parking garage.

Feet pounding the pavement, he heard Ryan yelling at him to stop. But he couldn't. He had to find the shooter. His military training kicked in and he zigzagged across the open street to hit the parking garage where the shots had come from. He expected to feel a bullet slam into him and was almost surprised when it didn't happen.

Ryan's shouts still rang in his ears. But he couldn't stop now. He hit the parking garage full-on, weapon drawn. Fortunately, it was mostly empty.

Breaths coming in pants, he scanned the first floor, then headed for the second. Footsteps behind him made him spin.

"Ryan."

The fury in his brother's eyes didn't faze him. The sudden sounds of sirens in the distance didn't stop him. The law enforcement officers descending upon the garage didn't deter him.

He wanted his life back and he was going to go get it.

Demi felt the hand on her shoulder and turned, thinking Charles had returned through the back door. Instead, she came face-to-face with Alan Gregor. "What are you doing here?" she nearly shrieked. "Are you crazy? Someone's shooting at us!"

"I know." Sweat dripped from his brow. "I knew you were coming here and wanted to be here for you. But I knew you were with…him."

"Then why are you here now?" She flicked her gaze toward the door where Charles and Ryan had disappeared. Still no sign of the men—or the shooter.

Alan was saying, "I wanted to be here for you, Demi. I...well, it was my place to be the support you needed. So, I came anyway." He licked his lips and swiped at the sweat running down a ruddy cheek. "But when I got here, I couldn't make up my mind whether I should come in or not. Then the bullets started flying. I had to get in here and make sure you were okay."

She couldn't be too upset with the man. It wasn't his fault she couldn't remember him. She thought it touching that he would risk his life to help her.

Sirens sounded, lights flashed. Law enforcement descended upon the hotel and the surrounding area.

He grabbed her hand. "Come on, let's find a better place to hide."

"No, I need to stay here. Charles and Ryan went after the shooter and I need to wait on them."

"And what if the shooter decides to come inside? What will you do then?"

He had a point.

Both men had left. But there'd been no more shots. Maybe they already had him in custody.

"The police are here now," she said. "I think we'll be safer in here than out there."

Alan's hands gripped her shoulders. "Come with me, please, Demi. I...I need you to."

His intensity shook her. Why was this so important to him? "Alan…"

Tears pooled in the man's eyes as they hunkered behind the overturned table. "I thought I'd lost you forever. Now I've found you and I need you to come with me. Let me keep you safe this time. Just…let me do that, will you?"

Her heart thudded. Compassion filled her along with the certainty of what she needed to do. She had to tell Alan she couldn't marry him. She needed to call off the engagement. But now definitely wasn't the time. And she wasn't going anywhere with Alan in spite of his apparent need to be her hero in this.

"Come out the back way," he was saying. "I think it's safe now."

She started to refuse, then paused. Officers would be out there. Maybe Charles and Ryan.

"All right," she agreed. "Let's go."

Demi let him lead her toward the back of the hotel. As they opened the door a SWAT member descended upon them. "Hands up, hands up!"

They threw their hands in the air and were led to a safe area.

Demi lowered her hands and Alan clutched one as he pulled the baseball cap lower on his forehead with the other. "They're going to want us to give statements."

Nodding, only half listening, Demi looked around,

taking in the chaotic sights and sounds surrounding her. Where was Charles? And Ryan?

Officers separated them as they questioned them. Demi gave the details she could remember even while her eyes scanned the area. Was the shooter gone? Had he managed to get away? Or had Charles and Ryan been able to get to him? Now that she was behind the police-erected safety barriers, she couldn't see the parking garage.

Please God, keep them safe.

Charles watched Ryan slink toward where he was sure the bullets had come from. Charles hung around the building, watching Ryan's back. His brother had finally convinced him that while Charles had training as a soldier, he wasn't a cop and couldn't go around acting like one.

But he didn't like it. The waiting, the watching was as nerve-racking here as it had been in Iraq. The familiar tension tightening his shoulders and the rock in his gut—that had started while in the service—returned with a vengeance.

"Clear!" Ryan called. "But he was here." Charles joined him at the edge of the wall of the parking garage. Bullet casings littered the area. A French fry nudged the wall and Charles looked at Ryan.

"Where's the nearest trash can?"

"Over there."

Charles walked over, covered his hand with his

shirt, and nudged the top off. It landed with a clatter. Looking inside, he saw several fast food wrappers and drink cups. "All of this needs to be gathered for evidence."

"The CSU team will get that."

Charles walked back to the where the shooter had made himself comfortable and pointed to the scrape on top of the wall. "Look. That's where he rested the weapon."

Ryan sighed and shook his head as he walked away to check out the rest of the area.

But something nagged at him. Again, he studied the surrounding area as the CSU team arrived. Ryan flashed his ID, indicated Charles was with him and the officers got to work.

Charles pulled out his phone and dialed Demi's cell number. It rang four times then went to voice mail. He frowned. Why wouldn't she answer? He tried again.

Again, no answer.

Had she been hurt and he hadn't realized it?

A restless need to get back to Demi washed over him. He looked around. There was nothing more he could do here anyway.

And still something wouldn't leave him alone. He looked at the French fry, the trash can, the wall the shooter had hid behind.

"He was waiting on us."

"What?" One of the officers looked up at him.

"He knew we were going to be here. But how?" Desperately, his mind tossed around conversations he'd had concerning the trip here. He couldn't remember who'd been around when they'd discussed it. But someone had found out and beat them here.

Ryan was deep in conversation with one of the SWAT members. He pointed at Charles who walked toward them.

"It's clear," the officer said. "Shooter fired several shots into the building. He was probably gone before we even got here."

"But why?" Charles asked, puzzled. "There was no way that bullet was going to come near me or anyone else."

"What was his purpose?"

"Who knows?" Charles ran a hand through his hair and looked around. "I thought it was because he followed us here. He thought he'd finally have a chance at me. But I don't think we were followed. I think he knew we'd be here." Charles explained his theory. "But you'd think he'd have picked a better spot. And why didn't he just pick me off as we walked into the hotel?"

"Because he's not after you."

"What?"

"He's after someone else. Demi."

Charles processed Ryan's words and horror hit him. "The shots were a distraction, is that what you're saying?"

"We've been concentrating so hard on who's after you that we've ignored the fact that someone broke into Demi's apartment and left the message."

"You don't belong here," Charles whispered, recalling the message. "Then someone believes she belongs somewhere else."

"And what better way to get to her than to get us out of the way?"

Without another word, the two men whirled and raced toward the now-cleared hotel building.

Charles burst through the shattered doors, the glass crunching under his feet.

His eyes swept the lobby.

Demi was gone.

NINETEEN

Demi answered the officer's questions as best she could, but she knew she wasn't much help. He finally let them go and she looked for Ryan and Charles to no avail.

Where had they gone? She knew they wouldn't just desert her. Were they hurt? Had they found the shooter?

"Demi, come with me," Alan insisted. "My car's over here."

"No, I need to wait for Charles—and Ryan," she said. "I can't just leave. I have to make sure they're all right."

"They're fine. And it's hot out here. If you want to wait for them, let's at least do it in air-conditioned comfort."

He took her upper arm and urged her to go with him. Looking around, she still didn't see the two men she wanted to see. "I'm not worried about being hot. I'm worried about Charles and Ryan."

She pulled away from his grasp and started to turn back the way they'd come.

Alan groaned and stumbled.

Demi stopped and spun to catch his arm. With a gasp, she asked, "Alan? Are you all right?"

"Everything all right?" Demi turned to see the officer who had questioned her. He stood there, his expression concerned. "Sir? You need some help?"

"I'm…diabetic," Alan said. "M…my medicine is in the car."

"I'll get one of the paramedics," Demi blurted out. She turned to go get help and he grabbed her arm, his fingers digging into her skin.

"No," he said. "Please, just help me get to the car and I'll be fine."

Demi cast another glance over her shoulder. Still no sign of Ryan and Charles, but she could no longer see the front of the hotel.

She looked back at Alan and thought he did look flushed. The sheen of sweat across his brow convinced her. "Okay, come on, we'll get your medicine and then I'll check on Charles and Ryan."

"Do you need any assistance?" the officer asked. "It's no trouble to get some medical help over here now."

"No," Alan insisted. "They're busy taking care of anyone who may have been hurt in the shooting. And really, I just need to get to my car and get my medicine. I'll be fine. I promise." He looked at Demi and licked his lips. "But we need to hurry. Please."

Torn, Demi knew she had to help Alan. "Sure. Sure. Let's get it and then I'm going to come back and check on Charles, all right?"

"Yes. Yes, that is fine. Thanks. It's in the glove compartment." He paused as they walked, Alan leaning heavy on her, his breathing ragged. "I'm sorry to put you out."

She took his hand. "It's no trouble." It was, but she couldn't refuse to help the man who'd gone to so much trouble to track her down.

"There," he pointed. "It's the Camry."

At the car, she opened the passenger door.

And felt a hard shove in the middle of her back. She landed face-first in the driver's seat. "Hey!" Turning, she came in contact with the barrel of a small gun.

Fear exploded in her chest. "Alan?" Disbelief shuddered through her. "What are you doing?"

"Move over," he growled. "Get in the driver's seat."

"No! What…"

His hand came back and slammed against her cheek. She cried out as pain shattered through her.

Along with her memories.

Darkness pressed in on her, but she fought it, re-fusing to give in and pass out. She needed to think. To remember. To focus.

Her mind spun, her breathing felt forced. And in that instant, clarity hit her.

Alan had done this to her.

And then she didn't have time to think of anything but surviving another attack by the man who'd beaten her and left her for dead. Ignoring the pain, she strived to gather her wits.

"Drive!" His furious shout in her right ear made her flinch. She grabbed the wheel and maneuvered behind it, her cheek throbbing.

Reaching over her, he jammed the keys into the ignition and cranked the car. "Now go!"

Demi put the vehicle in gear, but her hands shook too hard to grasp the steering wheel.

Alan muttered to himself as he glanced out the window, checked the rearview and side mirrors. Demi sat in stunned shock as she tried to sort through the sudden surge of memories, knowledge—and terror. She blinked as she remembered her loving parents. The home she'd grown up in. Friends she'd left in Brazil.

But along with those emotions came a rage like she'd never felt before. She'd been living in the hotel because Alan had scared her. He'd been persistent. Too persistent. When she'd come home to find him in her bedroom one Sunday afternoon, she'd realized something was wrong with the man.

Terror zipped through her.

As did a desperation to survive so she could be

with Charles. Make a life with him. Through teeth clenched against the pain, she asked, "Where do you want me to go?"

He jerked as though he had just realized they weren't moving. He looked around. "Shut up. Let me think."

She held her tongue. He started that crazy muttering again. "They're going to wonder where you are. They'll come to your house."

"My house?" She played dumb. "I have a house? Where?"

"But they don't know I was there, they don't know I was the shooter so they can't find me, they won't know where to look." His words jumbled together into one long sentence and it took an effort to not only hear what he was saying, but to understand it.

"You were the one shooting?" Hysteria bubbled near the surface and she pulled in a deep breath as they sat in the car in the middle of the parking lot.

Alan still muttered. "They never saw me, I made sure of that." He grabbed her bag, rummaged through it and then threw it in the back.

"What are you doing?"

"Shut up and drive."

She gulped and put the car in Drive. "You gave a statement, Alan. The officer saw me leave with you." Demi pulled into the traffic going in the opposite direction than where she thought he wanted her to go.

He hadn't noticed yet. He was still thinking. He grinned at her and she wondered why she hadn't noticed before now that his smiles never reached his eyes. He said, "The officer doesn't have any idea who I am. I didn't use my name."

More memories flooded her. After the bedroom incident, he'd sent her flowers. Bought her a puppy she'd insisted he take back to the pet store. As much as she loved animals, she had no place in her life for one. He'd been angry, yelled at her and called her ungrateful. Grabbed her, pulled her against him and told her that she belonged to him and she'd better get used to the idea.

Demi remembered the fear that had filled her at his words, the expression on his face—the bruises on her upper arms the next morning.

And knew he was dangerous.

Demi had decided to leave. To get away from the man until it was time for her to return to Brazil. So she'd checked into the hotel.

"Hey, where are you going?" Alan yelled now.

Demi cringed away from him, scared he would hit her again. "I don't know. You haven't said where to go. I'm just driving. I'll go wherever you want. Just tell me."

Her compliance seemed to calm him.

A little.

"Turn around. No, wait, just go to the next street and turn left. Then make another right."

"Where are you taking me? Why are you doing this?"

He sneered at her. "You're mine." Then his face softened and he reached out a hand to stroke her hair. "From the moment I saw you, talked to you in your parents' yard, I knew you were meant for me."

She gulped, tried not to pull away from the hand still caressing the back of her head and recalled the few conversations they'd had before he'd turned mental on her. He'd seemed kind enough, like an eager puppy who just wanted to be friends.

And then he'd asked her out.

She'd refused because she'd been planning to return to Brazil and hadn't wanted to start any kind of relationship with a man.

But that wasn't the only reason. As kind as he'd come across, she'd also sensed something, read something in his eyes that had set off her internal alarms. She'd used returning to her parents as an excuse not to go out with him.

He'd taken it well, she'd thought. How very wrong she was. "What made you decide you wanted me? Why me?"

"You were so kind, so gentle. So good with the children in the neighborhood. I watched how they'd run up to you and hug you." He swiped a hand across his face. "And you baked me cookies."

As a friendly gesture. Nothing more. Initially, he'd seemed lonely, sad, and she'd felt sorry for him. "You said you missed your mother's cooking. I was just trying to be nice, to be kind."

"And you were." From the corner of her eye, she saw his jaw tighten. She turned right. He continued. "You were nice. So very nice. Then I asked you out and you ran like a scared rabbit. I was so mad at myself for messing things up." He tapped the gun against the side of his head and let out a humorless chuckle. "Then it came to me. It wasn't me, it was you. You just didn't know what you were missing. You didn't realize that I was perfect for you. So, I decided to show you. But you wouldn't give me the chance to do it."

"Show me how, Alan?" She remembered her version, but wondered what he was thinking, wondered how his twisted mind interpreted her refusal to date him.

"I tried to convince you to go away with me. Just spend some time alone so you could get to know me. Again you refused. Said you could never go away with a man, that it wouldn't look right and you had to avoid all appearances of impropriety because of your job."

And because that's the way God had directed her to live her life.

Three weeks later, Alan had found her at the hotel. How he'd tracked her down, she wasn't sure, but he'd caught her as she'd been coming back from doing a load of laundry.

Her laundry. At the hotel. It had been folded neatly. She gulped. He'd folded her laundry. After he'd left her for dead. She didn't remember the whole attack, but she did remember the first few blows, the exploding pain. The realization that she knew the person attacking her. She remembered thinking she had to fight, to stay awake—or she'd never wake again.

Nausea swirled, her thoughts scattered at the memory and she wanted to scream.

Instead, she bit her tongue, forced her breathing to even out and ordered herself to stay calm. "I'm sorry. That doesn't sound very reasonable of me, does it?"

Satisfaction spread across his face. "Now you get it."

"You put that message in my coffee can, didn't you?"

He snickered. "Yeah."

"Why? What was the point?"

He frowned. "To show you that you didn't belong with that guy."

"Charles?"

"Yes," he snarled, then mocked. "Charles. I followed you, watching you mooning over him, acting all lovey-dovey. Smiling at him, helping him. That should have been me!" His fist slammed onto the dash and Demi jumped, the car swerving to the left. With effort, she pulled it back onto the road and bit her lip to keep the tears at bay.

Alan growled, "You belonged to me. Not him."

"I didn't remember, Alan. I didn't know," she whispered. Anything to settle him down. "Why didn't you just come up to me and tell me all of this when you found me?"

"I didn't know you had amnesia. The news didn't say anything about amnesia," he muttered.

He'd been afraid to approach her. Afraid she would recognize him and turn him into the police. But he'd approached her at the wedding reception.

"When did you realize I had amnesia?"

"I overheard some of the guests at the wedding talking about poor Charles's new and clueless nanny. When I asked what they meant, they were more than happy to fill me in."

And allowed him to come up with a plan to kidnap her.

She turned her gaze back to the road. "Where to now?"

"Make the third left up here."

"Where are we going?"

"We need to make a quick stop."

A stop? Excitement leaped inside her. Would she have a chance to escape?

He smirked. "And don't even think of trying to leave me again. If you do, I'll go straight back to

Fitzgerald Bay and kill every one of Charles Fitzgerald's precious family members. Including his two little brats."

Demi's heart sank. Would he really? Could he?

Yes, he would. She had no guarantee she could get to a phone fast enough to warn Charles and his family.

She was trapped.

"And then," Alan said gleefully, "we're going to my house—our house. The house where we'll live after we're married."

TWENTY

Charles was ready to punch something. "Where is she?"

His question met with silence.

Ryan's phone rang and he answered it. Charles moved in so he could hear and Ryan complied by pressing the speaker phone button.

Owen's voice came over the line. "Get this. Alan Gregor was indeed in Iraq, but his time line is off. His statement that he was a contractor was true, but he disappeared days before that IED exploded on the convoy. No one died, either. He was listed as AWOL. When they finally located him, they placed him in a mental institution. He just got out a few months ago."

Charles felt the blood drain from his face.

Ryan said, "Send me Alan's picture. I might need it."

"Sure thing."

"What else you got?"

"Nothing on Alan yet, but we released the information about that charm that was found at the crime scene where Olivia was killed."

"And?"

"We're hoping someone will recognize it and be able to tell us who it belongs to."

"But nothing yet?"

"No. That piece of the puzzle is still missing."

Missing along with someone he loved. The silent admission didn't even surprise. Yes, he loved Demi. And she'd told him that she loved him, too.

At first, the words had rocked him, but even as he'd struggled to absorb what that meant, he knew without a doubt that he wanted a future with her.

And now she was missing. The fact that something may have happened to her sent terror shooting through him.

Charles did his best to calm his fears as he cut his eyes to Ryan. "We can worry about all that later. I have a bad feeling about the danger Demi is in and we need to find her now."

Ryan said, "Be prepared to get down here, Owen. Something's going on and I have a feeling things are going to get dicey." He hung up and looked at Charles. "Let's ask around, see if we can figure out who she left with."

After questioning several people, they finally hit pay dirt when they approached the officer in charge of the scene and showed him Demi's picture. "Have you seen this woman?" Charles asked.

"Yeah, she was here a little while ago." The man's name tag read R. Luther.

Excitement leaped inside Charles. "Did you see where she went?"

Officer Luther's eyes squinted as he took another look at the picture Charles had on his phone. "Yeah, she got in a car with some guy. I remember because the guy looked like he might have been sick, was leaning on her pretty heavy. Think he said he was diabetic. I offered to get some medical help for him, but he said he had a kit in his car and would be fine. I was needed over here so I left them to it."

Charles felt slightly better. "That sounds like Demi. If someone needed help, she'd be the first one to offer. But why would she get in his car? And why wouldn't she call me and let me know what she was doing?" He looked at Ryan, his heart still troubled. "She would know I would be worried about her. This is really out of character for her."

"Sorry, can't help you with that," Officer Luther said. He paused then rubbed his chin and said, "It was kind of weird, though."

"What was?" Charles demanded.

The officer shrugged. "I turned back just for a second look to make sure he hadn't passed out or anything and noticed she got in the passenger side then slid over to the driver's seat."

Ryan and Charles exchanged another look. Ryan

said, "You're right, that's weird. I don't like the sound of that."

"I mean she could have been trying to help, get the kit, and he asked her to drive him to the hospital for all I know," Luther said. "But I remember thinking it was kind of strange. Then my boss called and I got distracted." He grimaced. "Sorry."

Ryan shook his head. "The only reason I can think of for that kind of maneuver is if he was forcing her to go with him."

Charles's relief morphed back into worry. He looked at the officer. "Did you see a weapon?"

"No." He frowned. "But that doesn't mean he didn't have one."

"What kind of car was he driving?"

The officer rubbed his eyes then said, "I'm not sure. Some kind of sedan." He sighed. "Look, I'm sorry, things were crazy over here and I had already talked to those two, my boss was calling…" He trailed off, glanced back where the car had been then said, "It was blue, I do remember that."

Charles felt his heart skip a beat. Then had a wild idea. To Ryan, he said, "Show him the picture of Alan."

With a raised brow, Ryan asked, "You think she could have left with him?"

"I don't know. But I do know that he's unhinged and he wants Demi. Can't hurt to ask."

Ryan complied. "Was this the guy she was with?"

Officer Luther nodded. "Yeah, that could be him. He had on a baseball cap, but yeah…it looks like him." Then he frowned again as he pulled out a little notebook. He flipped a few pages then said, "But his name wasn't Alan. He said his name was Christopher Holden."

"I don't like this," Charles stated. "Something's not right with this."

"I agree." Ryan nodded, his eyes troubled.

"We need to track them down. And fast."

Ryan's gaze rested on the corner of the bank's building. "We've got all the footage of the shooting from the video cameras. Now we need to watch them again and see if we can get a plate off the car Demi got into."

"Where was the car parked?" Ryan asked the officer.

Officer Luther pointed. "Over there in that lot across the street, somewhere around the middle. I watched them for a little while to make sure he didn't collapse and need more help. But they made it to the car fine."

Ryan nodded his thanks then said to Charles, "Let's go watch that footage." He snagged a uniformed officer. "Do you mind checking that parking lot for a camera?" He explained in detail the area he particularly wanted to know about.

Five minutes later, in the security office of the hotel, Charles stood behind his brother while Ryan scanned the footage, running it through to the appropriate time. And then he pointed. "There she is. Demi and someone exiting the building. But it's from the back."

"And now they're out of range. They're off the camera." Ryan slapped his thigh in disgust.

Charles felt his fear blossom. How was he going to find Demi?

Prayers formed on his lips even as he kept his eyes on the next camera.

The officer Ryan had sent to check on the camera in the parking lot came in, phone tucked against his ear. "I've got it. They're in a blue Camry." He looked at Charles as he bolted to his feet, ready for action when Ryan pointed to the video that was now being fed to the monitor he watched. He said, "It looks like he forced her into the car."

"We've got to get her. Now," Charles barked. "How are we going to find her?"

"I've already got a trace on her cell phone." He looked at Charles. "You got her a good one. The GPS is on and we're tracking them now. And I've got a helicopter on the way."

Charles felt the tightness in his chest ease slightly. Demi was still in the hands of a madman, but at least they had a way to find her.

Ryan listened a few more seconds then frowned. "They're stopped? Where?" He looked at Charles. "Dedham."

Charles said, "You need to get the local police to the location."

"On it," Ryan said.

Charles paced, feeling like he should be doing something. Why would Alan take her to Dedham? Dedham was a small town, even smaller than Fitzgerald Bay.

Where strangers would stand out. Alan had to know that the authorities would put Demi's picture on the news again once they realized she was missing.

"That's not right," he said. "That's not them. He wouldn't just drive thirty miles then stop."

"Maybe he's not done. Maybe he's just stopped for gas or something."

"No, it doesn't make sense."

"He's not going to act or think like a rational human being. He's unpredictable," Owen agreed.

Charles gulped. "Which makes him all the more dangerous."

"Exactly."

Charles felt helpless. He paced, his limp more pronounced. The way it always got when he was under a lot of stress. Ignoring it, he ran a hand through his hair and then finally stopped, dropped his chin to his chest and sighed. *God, please be there for Demi. I don't know what's going on with her or where she is, but please keep her safe.*

"How close are the local police?" Charles asked. He paced forward, then back in the small room.

Ryan relayed the question. "They're there. They've tracked her cell phone to a car." He paused as he listened. "But it's a black Honda driven by a couple in their sixties."

Charles's head snapped up. "He knew we'd track her. Alan slipped her phone into another car." Now the fear swamped him, threatening to suffocate him. "Why didn't she get away from him before now?" he murmured. "Does he have her tied up?" The thought sickened him and he forced himself not to dwell on those kinds of thoughts.

"I've got the airport covered, the major bus lines, the train station. I've got a BOLO out on his Camry." Ryan shook his head. "We'll just have to see what comes in."

"No." Charles refused to accept the wait-and-see attitude. "This guy was in a mental hospital. He's not thinking right—or straight." Charles closed his eyes and pulled on every bit of psychology he'd ever studied. "He'll want to go somewhere familiar, somewhere comfortable. If he's been fixated on Demi, he'll take her to a place that has meaning to him."

"Where? His home?"

Charles nodded. "Yes, that's the first place we need to look."

"But where does he live?"

"He was her next-door neighbor," Charles whispered. "Go to Demi's address in Springfield and we'll find Alan's house."

Ryan shook his head but didn't disagree. He just said, "It's a long shot."

"I know it is. But it's the only shot we've got right now."

Demi squirmed in her seat, desperate for an opening. She had to get away from Alan or she wouldn't live to see nightfall.

Unless she went along with him. Possibly. But it would take all her acting skills and she didn't know if she could do it.

But she had to.

If she wanted to live.

She looked at him. "Where were we going to live after we were married?"

Alan's gaze shot to her. "Keep your eyes on the road."

Demi complied. He continued, "In my house, of course." From the corner of her eye, she saw his jaw tightened. "Pretty soon you'll forget all about that

Charles guy and we'll start a family and live like we were meant to live."

Demi swallowed hard. He was delusional. Did he really think it was possible to do that? She looked at him again then quickly back in front of her. "I don't know, Alan. It's pretty hard to just pick up with someone you don't even remember."

His hand reached out to stroke her cheek and she forced herself not to cringe from him. Instead, she swallowed the sudden nausea and concentrated on driving. "Where do I go now?"

She didn't want to let on that she'd regained her memory. There was no telling how that would affect him. Her cheek throbbed a steady beat, a reminder that she was in the company of a vicious man.

"Just keep going on this road. I'll give you plenty of notice where to turn."

"Okay." Her easy agreement seemed to calm him and Demi drew in a steadying breath. As long as she was driving, she was alive.

Where was Charles? She glanced in the rearview mirror as though she expected to see him behind her. Cars passed her on the left and she had a white Chevy behind, but none of them were the red truck she longed to see. Then again, if he realized what had happened to her, he might be riding with someone else.

Her heart-sent prayers to the one she knew could deliver her from this situation. *Please, Lord, let*

Charles find me. Provide a way for me to escape. I love Charles, Lord, and believe You sent me to him and his family for a reason. Please, please, deliver me from this man.

She drove and prayed and Alan fell silent. She knew where she was going. He was taking her to her home. Only she knew it wouldn't be to her parents' house.

It would be to his.

But hope swelled. Charles knew where she lived. He would be looking for her. Maybe when Charles arrived, she could signal him somehow. Let him know she was next door. Her mind clicked with everything she could try. Devising plan after plan, she discarded one after the other.

After another forty-five minutes of silence, Alan perked up. "Get off at this exit then make a left at the stop sign."

She did. They were about ten minutes from their destination. She checked the rearview mirror again. Still no sign of Charles—or anyone else—looking for her.

Her knotted stomach twisted into a solid ball of fear.

"Slow down. Turn here."

A helicopter thumped overhead and Demi felt a leap in her pulse. Could it be searching for her? Alan tensed and stuck his head out the window to stare at the chopper.

The chopper hovered for a brief moment then it banked right and flew off.

Alan relaxed back into the seat and gave a low chuckle.

Tears threatened again.

She'd held her fear in so tight and now that they were almost to Alan's house, she felt like she might explode. And then she was in the driveway. Turning, she begged, "Please, Alan, let me go. Do you really want to be with someone who doesn't want to be with you?"

The fist that cracked against her face seemed to come from nowhere.

Darkness blanketed her.

TWENTY-ONE

"We've got them," Ryan reported from the backseat. "The helicopter spotted the car. Demi was driving and Alan stuck his head out of the window to stare up at the helicopter so the pilot peeled off. But he circled back to see the vehicle turn into the subdivision. The car is now in the garage."

He'd been right. Charles sat in the passenger seat of Owen's car and felt some of the horrid fear ease somewhat. They knew where she was. Now they just had to get her away from that madman without him killing her.

Charles looked at Owen who was driving. "Can't this thing go any faster?"

"I'm already doing a hundred." The blue lights swirled on the dash and Charles felt the seat belt cut into his shoulder as he leaned forward.

"We're not going to get there any faster by you giving yourself a heart attack. Sit back and try to get your blood pressure under control."

Good advice from his brother, but an impossible feat.

He did lean back, but his fists stayed clenched on his thighs. "I just want thirty seconds alone with him."

Owen nodded. "I know you do, but this guy doesn't fight fair."

Charles snorted. "I didn't exactly have fair in mind."

"Right."

Silence descended.

"Local police are at the scene," Ryan reported. "They're watching and waiting for us to arrive."

"Good," Owen said.

Charles asked, "Have they seen her? Can they get a look through the windows?"

"No, the blinds are pulled and there are heavy curtains over the blinds."

Charles continued his prayers as they pulled off on the exit that would lead them to Demi.

Demi groaned. Her head pounded into a migraine so fierce she thought she might die. Nausea swirled and she rolled to her side.

"Demi? Demi? I know you're awake. I've been watching you."

Memories returned full force. She knew who she was. She knew who Alan Gregor was.

And she knew she was going to die today.

But the way her head felt, dying might be a relief.

Something cool touched her lips.

Water. She took a sip, then another. It tasted bitter and she grimaced. Her stomach rebelled.

Demi let out another pained groan and lay back as gently as possible. "My head," she whispered.

"I know. But that will pass. I put a mild narcotic in there to help with the pain." A cool cloth touched her forehead, covered her eyes and for a moment she panicked, but it felt so good, she decided to leave it there. Alan continued in what he probably thought was his soothing voice. "I didn't want to hit you. But you just made me so mad when you asked me to let you go that I decided you needed some severe discipline in order for you to understand."

Understand? Understand what?

"Because I will never let you go. And if you ask me again, I will punish you again. Are we clear?"

"Yes," she said simply.

The headache receded from migraine to just really bad.

"Good." He sounded satisfied.

"It was you all along," she whispered. "You were the one in the gray hoodie."

"Yes. I tracked you down and was determined to bring you back here. Where you belong. You didn't belong there."

"And that night, in the bookstore. That was you, too?"

"Yes again. Only I wasn't fast enough. I didn't know the layout of the store and you got away from me. Then cops got there so fast…" She could almost picture him shrugging, but didn't want to open her eyes yet. He said, "And yes, that was my message in the church where you were looking all lovey-dovey at Fitzgerald."

The hard tone returned to his voice and she knew she needed to get him talking about something else. "Tell me about my parents."

"I've never met them. One day, once you've accepted your position here with me, I will allow you to introduce us."

The nausea faded a bit and she pulled in a relieved breath.

"You have some color back in your cheeks. Feeling better?" he asked.

"No."

A quiet sigh filtered to her ears. "I'll give you a few more minutes, then we can talk again."

Talking was about the last thing she wanted to do right now.

Unless it was with Charles.

She heard Alan's footsteps recede then the quiet click of the door.

The slamming of the dead bolt jolted her and the cloth slipped from her eyes onto the bed where she lay. Still she kept her eyes shut.

Her entire face hurt. Her cheek, her jaw. Her head. Everything.

Going by feel, she picked up the cloth and placed

it against her throbbing cheek. With every heartbeat, pain pulsed.

But she couldn't lie there. She needed to find a way out of—

Where was she?

Pulling the cloth from her eyes, she squinted, wincing at the shaft of agony caused by the light.

Ignoring the pain, she sat up and did her best to take in her surroundings.

She was in a bedroom. Whose? Alan's? She shuddered. The furniture appealed to her taste, though. Not terribly masculine, but not overly feminine, either. Demi had the awful thought that he'd actually picked it out with her in mind. Another shiver racked her.

She frowned and let her eyes wander from the dresser to the door.

Then back to the window.

She slid gently from the bed, keeping one hand on the edge to keep her balance. Standing, she swayed, caught herself then stayed still until the room stopped spinning and the lightning-sharp pain dulled to a jackhammer throb.

"Please, Lord…" she whispered as she stumbled to the window. "Please let me see Charles again."

She yanked back the curtain—and stared at a cement wall. A sob threatened to break through. She swallowed it and pulled the curtain again into place.

Vaguely, she wondered if Alan could see her. Was he monitoring her with hidden cameras?

She decided she didn't care. She moved to one of the two doors and twisted the knob. The door opened easily and her heart leaped. Then sank to her toes when she stepped into a bathroom. She turned in a circle taking in the perfectly matched towels, little soaps on the sink and the exact brand of facial cleanser that she used.

She stepped away and felt the wall touch her back. Sliding down to the floor, she rested her aching forehead on her bent knees and sobbed.

Charles felt every muscle in his body go rigid when they pulled onto the street where Demi was being held. Still no sighting or any activity had been reported. Charles continued to pray.

They parked and Ryan said, "Stay here."

"Not a chance." Charles didn't wait for permission. He'd been trained to fight, to face his battles. He'd even been involved in rescuing a fellow marine who'd been captured and held hostage by a group of Iraqi refugees.

And he had his weapon.

Ryan didn't argue with him. Instead, his brother approached the command truck that had parked out of sight of the house. Charles followed him.

Once inside the van, Ryan introduced himself to

the man in charge, Detective Pierce Sands. Ryan asked him, "Anything?"

Detective Sands shook his head. "I've got a SWAT team on the way. We're getting our equipment in place to get eyes and ears in there. Right now, I have orders to let you be the lead on this since you know the suspect and the victim."

Charles watched the action for a few moments, then turned to study the house. It was an older home, probably thirty to forty years old. From the front, it looked like a single-story house, but he'd overheard Ryan talking about the layout and knew it had a basement. The house next door was Demi's parents' house. The house she'd grown up in. He wondered if it had triggered any memories when she'd seen it.

The small utility shed next to Alan's house looked strange. Out of place. Who put a utility shed *beside* his house? But Alan had proved he wasn't stable and Charles longed to rush the house and pull Demi from that madman's clutches.

Action erupted.

The SWAT team had arrived.

Charles watched as officers swarmed toward the house in silent fashion planting themselves around the perimeter. Alan would not be getting out of that house through any of the doors or windows.

Charles stepped out of the van and watched, praying Demi was all right.

One of the officers with a megaphone yelled, "Alan Gregor, we have you surrounded. Let your hostage go and come out of the house."

Charles waited for a response.

Nothing.

Would he harm Demi when he realized he had nowhere to go?

Gut in a knot, heart beating fast enough to make him light-headed, Charles continued to watch. And wait.

"How did they find me!" Alan screamed as the door to her prison slammed open. Demi held herself rigid. If he hit her again, she wouldn't be able to function. She was barely managing it now.

Passing out would not help the situation. Alan paced, the gun held at his side. He turned on her. "How did they know?" His eyes narrowed and he lifted the gun to point it at her. "You told them."

Demi's heart fluttered. Fear strangled her. "How would I do that, Alan? You threw my cell phone away and I've been with you since we left. I didn't tell them anything, I promise. And remember? The night of the reception? You told me we were neighbors. Charles was sitting there listening." She kept her words calm, praying they were the right words and wouldn't send him off on another tangent.

He stopped. "I did?" Then he gripped his head with both hands, the gun mashed against his skull.

"No, I didn't! I wouldn't say that!" He calmed so fast she blinked. He said, "But you're right. You couldn't tell them. And you wouldn't, would you? Because you want to be with me, right?"

"Right." She swallowed hard at the lie and then took a chance. "Do you want me to tell them to go away? That I'm here because I want to be?"

He jerked. "You would do that?"

"If it would help, I would." Help her get out of here.

He walked over and grabbed her upper arm and yanked her toward the door. "Stay in front of me."

She obeyed, climbing the stairs, her heart beating fast as she could almost taste her freedom.

One thing for sure, she wasn't going back down those steps alive.

At the top, they turned left and he steered her with a rough hand toward the front door. "They've got me surrounded," he hissed. "I know how this works. The only way I'm going to get out of this is if you make them believe you want to be here."

She stayed calm, heart racing, knowing that Charles was probably somewhere outside the door. She knew that with all her heart.

The phone rang and Alan jerked. The movement jarred her head and she winced. He either didn't notice or didn't care. "Answer it."

She reached out a shaking hand. "Hello?"

"Is this Demi?"

"Yes, Ryan, hi. It's good to hear your voice."

"Are you all right?"

With a look at Alan's wild eyes, Demi forced a lightness into her voice. "Of course I'm all right."

"Is he listening in?"

Demi flicked a glance at Alan whose eyes roamed the room, never resting, never still. She needed to send a message to Ryan. What could she say? "No, no, I assure you, I'm fine. How are you?"

"He's not listening."

"That's right, we just got here a few minutes ago."

A pause. "My sniper needs a visual. The den blinds are partially open. Can you maneuver Alan in front of them?"

"I don't know. Possibly."

"Tell me where he's standing, can you do that?"

Alan gestured for her to give him the phone.

She hurried to say, "Sure, but um…he wants to talk to you."

Demi held out the phone to her kidnapper and he snatched it from her. "Hello?" He paused and frowned. Then said, "She's here because she wants to be. No, you can't speak to her again. You've already heard that she's fine." Alan listened a few more minutes then rolled his eyes with a huff. "Here, she'll tell you one more time, then you leave. Right?"

Demi took the phone back and pressed it against her ear. "Yes, I want to be here."

Alan motioned with the gun and hissed. "Tell them something useful. Convince them you want to be here."

She nodded and swallowed hard. Holding the handset, she moved toward the den area, the open blinds Ryan had mentioned. Alan stayed right on her, following her, lapping up her words. "I...I mean, why wouldn't I? He's got a beautiful kitchen with granite countertops." Alan's chest puffed a bit and he smiled, nodding his approval. She moved again and so did Alan. "And he's obviously spent time caring for the place." She hitched a breath as Alan moved closer, his smile growing. Demi touched the mantel, praising the craftsmanship. Alan backed up and let her regale them with what a good job he'd done with the house.

"And the...uh...window in the living area is just gorgeous. I know you can't see in because of the drapes, but about two feet to *your* left is Alan's... um, his favorite painting." Would they get it? Couldn't they see him by now? She continued. "And I'm just loving it because from where I'm standing over near the fireplace, I can see..."

The window she'd just described exploded.

Alan screamed and went down.

The front door imploded and Demi launched herself toward it.

"Demi!" Alan's yell of fury propelled her faster.

And then she slipped.

She felt her neck jerk in a whiplash as Alan's hand snagged itself in her hair. Pain like she'd only felt the night Alan had beat her and left her for dead ricocheted through her. The men in the SWAT gear with rifles pointed faded from her vision.

Alan jammed the gun against the side of her head and everyone froze. Without a word to the men yelling at him to put the gun down, he started backing up. A warm wetness soaked into the back of her right shoulder.

Alan had been shot, but not bad enough to slow him down.

His ragged breathing echoed in her ear. He called her a few choice names then told her, "Keep going. Into the kitchen. Should have just done this to begin with, but I was hoping you could convince them… make them go away…leave us alone. Now we're going to be running forever. Stupid. Stupid."

"Alan, please…" She tried to interrupt his senseless mutterings.

The pressure of the barrel increased. "Move. Now." She backed up like he'd ordered.

Into the large walk-in pantry.

Charles held back and watched, weapon ready as the SWAT team flooded the house. He's heard the scream as the shot entered the window, but now he could make no sense of the jumble of yells coming from inside the house.

He itched to be in the middle of it and for the first time since returning from Iraq, he wished he'd joined the police force.

"Come on, come on."

Then he heard, "He's gone!"

Charles froze. No. He was in there. They'd talked to Demi, taken her cue and shot through the window where she had told them to shoot.

Charles looked at the house next door. Demi's house.

And saw movement from the shed.

The door opened and Charles saw Alan push Demi in front of him out into the sunlight.

He raced toward them, weapon pointed, just as two SWAT team members saw them, too. Charles hollered, "Freeze, Alan!"

Alan whirled and yanked Demi in front of him.

Demi saw Charles sprinting for them. Felt the barrel of the gun back against her head.

And had had enough. "No!" she cried as she went limp.

The move pulled Alan off balance. Her hair felt like it was being pulled out by the roots.

More gunshots echoed around her and then silence.

"Demi!"

"Charles," she whispered. Why did he sound so far away?

She felt his arms go around her and pull her away from Alan's dead body.

TWENTY-TWO

Charles held her against him, his heart racing. "Demi," he whispered against her battered cheek.

She wilted and if he hadn't had his arms around her, she would have hit the ground. Paramedics on standby now rushed to Demi.

"Ma'am? Can we check you out?"

Charles wanted to tell them he'd do it himself, that he never wanted to let her go, but she pulled away and sank onto the gurney one of the paramedics had rolled toward him.

"He just hit me. It'll heal," she said, her voice dull, defeated.

"I'm a doctor. She needs X-rays," Charles insisted.

The man nodded. "I agree. We'll transport her."

"I'm going with you." Charles climbed in the back and let the one paramedic do his job while the other drove. Charles watched Demi, concerned with her silence, the empty look in her eyes.

But the fact that she held his hand with no apparent inclination to let go gave him hope.

Once Demi was settled in at the emergency department, Charles waited outside the curtain. A rather new and unsettling experience for him. In the future he vowed to have a little more compassion for those waiting on this side.

"How is she?"

Owen's voice intruded and Charles turned to find Ryan with him. "Hey, she's all right, I think. Thanks for everything you guys did."

Ryan slapped Charles on the back. "You're the hero. You're the one who spotted them coming out of the shed."

Owen shook his head. "Who would have figured? He had a set of stairs leading from the pantry in the kitchen, down then over and back up into the shed. Very weird dude."

"I thought that shed looked out of place where it was located, but…" Charles glanced toward the curtain that sheltered Demi. "It doesn't matter now. I'm just glad she's all right."

Owen looked at Ryan. "You want to tell him or you want me to?"

Charles lifted a brow. "Tell me what?"

Ryan said, "You've been cleared in Olivia's murder."

At first, Charles couldn't move. Then relief exploded through him as he said, "What? How? When?"

"Today. Dad called while we were headed over here. We filled him in on all the excitement then he said the DNA report came back. There were two different DNA samples on the rock that was found at the murder scene. The one that's been labeled the murder weapon. One of them was a match for Olivia's DNA, the other one is definitely not yours."

Charles wasn't sure what to say, what to think. For so long, the word *murderer* had been an albatross around his neck.

"Thanks, guys."

"Expect to be flooded with apologies by Fitzgerald Bay residents," Ryan said. "By Meghan Henry, too."

Charles felt months of tension leave his shoulders. Before anyone could speak, the doctor stepped from behind the curtain. "You can see her now, Charles."

"Thanks." Charles looked at his brothers. "Excuse me."

Then he was standing by Demi's bed. She had her eyes closed, her head turned away from him.

"Demi?" She rolled her head to look at him and he gave an inward wince at her battered face. He took her hand. "Hi."

She blinked up at him and licked her lips. "Who are you?"

Charles's heart hit his toes—until he saw the twinkle in her green eyes. He groaned. "You got me."

Her lips twitched. "I'm sorry, I couldn't resist."

He leaned over and planted a kiss on her lips. A soft, lingering kiss filled with all the love bursting through his heart.

She gave a small sigh as he pulled away. Then she frowned. "How can you stand to look at me? I resemble some horror-movie monster."

Through the lump in his throat, he said, "You're the most beautiful woman in the world to me."

Demi felt the tears leak from the corners of her eyes. "I love you, Charles," she whispered.

"I love you, Demi." He gave a low chuckle. "I can't believe I'm saying those words, but I mean each one of them."

Brilliant joy erupted within her. "I want to call my parents."

He grinned. "I already did."

"What do you mean?"

He flushed and looked so much like Aaron, she lifted a brow then winced at the move. Still, she asked, "Charles, what did you do?"

"I…um…asked your father for permission to marry you."

Demi felt her breath catch and for a long moment she stared into those gorgeous blue eyes. "Really?"

"Really."

"What did he say?" She couldn't imagine. Her father was her protector, the man she'd looked up to all her life. What would he say about her marrying a man she'd only known for a short time. A man her parents hadn't even met yet?

"He said he'd let me know after he met me. Then I happened to mention I had two-year-old twins and he offered to bring the minister to the house."

Demi burst out laughing then groaned as her head reminded her that wasn't a good move. But it didn't diminish her joy one bit. "They've dreamed of grandchildren for a long time." She blinked at the sudden surge of tears and whispered, "I can't believe this is happening."

Charles gently sat beside her on the bed and leaned over for another sweet kiss. Then he placed his forehead against hers, smiled into her eyes and whispered back, "Believe it."

* * * * *

Dear Reader,

Thank you so much for joining me on Demi and Charles's journey to find God and love for one another. This book is part of a continuity series so there was one issue that was left unresolved at the end of the story. I hope you'll find the last book and see how everything works out in the end. :)

As always, it's an honor to write these stories, to create the characters and breathe life into them. To watch them grow and learn as they deal with what life hands them. Truthfully, even though these characters aren't real, they still teach me! They remind me that God is an incredible God and that He loves me unconditionally. I need that reminder often! I pray that if you're going through a tough time right now, that you will cling to God and let Him walk with you through it.

Until next time, God Bless,

Lynette Eason

Questions for Discussion

1. Demi works for Charles and is warned about him being a suspect in a murder investigation. Do you think she was foolish to take the job without knowing for sure whether he killed his former nanny or not?

2. Charles's wife left him when things got too hard. Instead of sticking around and trying to work things out, she ran. What do you do when things get hard? Who do you turn to?

3. What was your favorite scene in this book? Why?

4. What did you think of Demi's decision not to get involved with Charles while she still didn't know her identity? Did you think it made sense? Why?

5. Demi wasn't sure how she felt about God simply because she couldn't remember whether she believed in Him or not. Yet her first inclination was to pray. Do you find that believable? Why or why not?

6. Demi is overwhelmed by the large Fitzgerald family and yet she wants to belong. Have you

ever felt like an outsider looking in? What was your reaction?

7. What do you think about someone who is so obsessed with his own world, his own goals that it doesn't matter who he hurts in his quest to achieve those goals? Do you know anyone like this?

8. Was there a character in the book that you identified with more than the others? If so, who and why?

9. Charles desperately wanted to do the right thing by Demi and not start a relationship with her and yet he couldn't stop himself from falling in love with her. In spite of his feelings, however, he acted honorably. What do you think of his actions? Do you agree he did the right thing?

10. Do you think Demi was a brave, courageous woman? Or just lost?

11. When Alan appeared in the picture, Demi was stunned. Charles wasn't happy, either. He thought he was going to lose Demi and that scared him. Have you ever felt that you were going to lose someone you loved to another person? What did you do about it?

12. Demi was upset with Alan's appearance, but she was excited, too, because Alan knew her, her identity. Do you blame her for wanting to talk with Alan? Spend time with him? What would you have done if you'd been in Demi's shoes?

13. Alan played on Demi's sympathies to get her into his car. Do you think she should have been more careful or would you have done the same thing if you'd been in her place?

14. When Charles realizes that Demi's been kidnapped and that she's in physical danger, he's determined to save her. And yet, he's not the police. He's frustrated because he feels like his hands are tied. Can you think of anything Charles could have done differently?

15. When Charles's wife left him, he turned from God. He wasn't necessarily angry with God, just apathetic. And yet as the story progresses, we see God drawing Charles back to Himself. How is your relationship with God? Are you angry with Him? Apathetic toward Him? What can you do to draw nearer to Him today?

LARGER-PRINT BOOKS!

GET 2 FREE
LARGER-PRINT NOVELS
PLUS 2 FREE
MYSTERY GIFTS

Love Inspired.
SUSPENSE
RIVETING INSPIRATIONAL ROMANCE

Larger-print novels are now available...

YES! Please send me 2 FREE LARGER-PRINT Love Inspired® Suspense novels and my 2 FREE mystery gifts (gifts are worth about $10). After receiving them, if I don't wish to receive any more books, I can return the shipping statement marked "cancel". If I don't cancel, I will receive 4 brand-new novels every month and be billed just $4.99 per book in the U.S. or $5.49 per book in Canada. That's a saving of at least 23% off the cover price. It's quite a bargain! Shipping and handling is just 50¢ per book in the U.S. and 75¢ per book in Canada.* I understand that accepting the 2 free books and gifts places me under no obligation to buy anything. I can always return a shipment and cancel at any time. Even if I never buy another book, the two free books and gifts are mine to keep forever.

110/310 IDN FEH3

Name _____ (PLEASE PRINT)

Address _____ Apt. #

City _____ State/Prov. _____ Zip/Postal Code

Signature (if under 18, a parent or guardian must sign)

Mail to the **Reader Service:**
IN U.S.A.: P.O. Box 1867, Buffalo, NY 14240-1867
IN CANADA: P.O. Box 609, Fort Erie, Ontario L2A 5X3

Not valid for current subscribers to Love Inspired Suspense larger-print books.

**Are you a current subscriber to Love Inspired Suspense books
and want to receive the larger-print edition?
Call 1-800-873-8635 or visit www.ReaderService.com.**

* Terms and prices subject to change without notice. Prices do not include applicable taxes. Sales tax applicable in N.Y. Canadian residents will be charged applicable taxes. Offer not valid in Quebec. This offer is limited to one order per household. All orders subject to credit approval. Credit or debit balances in a customer's account(s) may be offset by any other outstanding balance owed by or to the customer. Please allow 4 to 6 weeks for delivery. Offer available while quantities last.

Your Privacy—The Reader Service is committed to protecting your privacy. Our Privacy Policy is available online at www.ReaderService.com or upon request from the Reader Service.

We make a portion of our mailing list available to reputable third parties that offer products we believe may interest you. If you prefer that we not exchange your name with third parties, or if you wish to clarify or modify your communication preferences, please visit us at www.ReaderService.com/consumerschoice or write to us at Reader Service Preference Service, P.O. Box 9062, Buffalo, NY 14269. Include your complete name and address.

LISUSLP11B

LARGER-PRINT BOOKS!

**GET 2 FREE
LARGER-PRINT NOVELS
PLUS 2 FREE
MYSTERY GIFTS**

Love Inspired

Larger-print novels are now available...

YES! Please send me 2 FREE LARGER-PRINT Love Inspired® novels and my 2 FREE mystery gifts (gifts are worth about $10). After receiving them, if I don't wish to receive any more books, I can return the shipping statement marked "cancel". If I don't cancel, I will receive 6 brand-new novels every month and be billed just $4.99 per book in the U.S. or $5.49 per book in Canada. That's a saving of at least 23% off the cover price. It's quite a bargain! Shipping and handling is just 50¢ per book in the U.S. and 75¢ per book in Canada.* I understand that accepting the 2 free books and gifts places me under no obligation to buy anything. I can always return a shipment and cancel at any time. Even if I never buy another book, the two free books and gifts are mine to keep forever.

122/322 IDN FEG3

Name	(PLEASE PRINT)
Address	Apt. #
City	State/Prov.	Zip/Postal Code

Signature (if under 18, a parent or guardian must sign)

Mail to the **Reader Service:**
IN U.S.A.: P.O. Box 1867, Buffalo, NY 14240-1867
IN CANADA: P.O. Box 609, Fort Erie, Ontario L2A 5X3

Not valid to current subscribers to Love Inspired Larger-Print books.

**Are you a current subscriber to Love Inspired books
and want to receive the larger-print edition?
Call 1-800-873-8635 or visit www.ReaderService.com.**

* Terms and prices subject to change without notice. Prices do not include applicable taxes. Sales tax applicable in N.Y. Canadian residents will be charged applicable taxes. Offer not valid in Quebec. This offer is limited to one order per household. All orders subject to credit approval. Credit or debit balances in a customer's account(s) may be offset by any other outstanding balance owed by or to the customer. Please allow 4 to 6 weeks for delivery. Offer available while quantities last.

Your Privacy—The Reader Service is committed to protecting your privacy. Our Privacy Policy is available online at www.ReaderService.com or upon request from the Reader Service.

We make a portion of our mailing list available to reputable third parties that offer products we believe may interest you. If you prefer that we not exchange your name with third parties, or if you wish to clarify or modify your communication preferences, please visit us at www.ReaderService.com/consumerschoice or write to us at Reader Service Preference Service, P.O. Box 9062, Buffalo, NY 14269. Include your complete name and address.

LILP11B